Copyright © 2018 by Ashe Moon

2023 - 2nd Edition

All rights reserved. No part of this publication may be reproduced, distributed, or transmitted in any form or by any means, including photocopying, recording, or other electronic or mechanical methods, without the prior written permission of the publisher, except in the case of brief quotations embodied in critical reviews and certain other noncommercial uses permitted by copyright law.

BOUND TO THE OMEGA

THE LUNA BROTHERS MPREG ROMANCE SERIES

Stay updated with sales and new releases by subscribing to Ashe Moon's personal newsletter! Scan the QR code below with your phone camera!

* * *

If you're looking for something a little more personal you can also join my private Facebook group, **Ashe Moon's Ashetronauts**!

My group is a safe space to chat with me and other readers, and where I also do special exclusive giveaways and announcements. Hope to see you there!

THE LUNA BROTHERS SERIES

Loch's Story - Wed to the Omega
Vander's Story - Doctor to the Omega
Christophe's Story - Marked to the Omega

ARTHUR

The shock of cold fingers coming to rest on my bare abdomen snapped me unwelcomely out of my sleep. I turned my head and my face fell into a mess of tangled brown hair that was not my own. A beam of morning sunlight shone through a gap in the curtain, somehow managing to spotlight just my eyes. I squinted, cringing. In the confusion of my rude arousal, it took me a moment to remember just who it was that I was sharing my bed with, and with some hesitation, I carefully parted the frazzled curtain to take a peek at her face.

As the fog of sleep cleared from my mind, the memories of the night before returned to me. *Ah, that's right.* Miss Melany Dewall, heiress of the Rose Claw Clan.

The very first time I'd met Melany, I was six years younger. It was at a family function, my parents had invited all the biggest wolf clans to attend, and I'd told myself I would have her—at least for a night. Certain circumstances ruined those prospects that night, so when she contacted me two days ago and told me she'd be coming through Wolfheart for a charity function, I'd nearly forgotten who she was. Seemed I'd made more of an impact on her than she had on me, but six years could do that, especially when there were so many other brunettes in between…

Melany snorted in her sleep. I was awake, fog cleared. Now that the chase was over, the thrill and all existing desire was fading at breakneck speed. I just wanted her out of my bed. I reached up to tap the touch panel on the headboard above my pillow, and electronic motors began to whirr, drawing open the curtains and flooding the room with light. I shifted my body to pull myself out of bed when Melany stirred, pushed her hair out of her face, and smiled at me.

"Good morning, darling," she said, and I cringed. *Darling?* No, no, no. Then I felt her fingers make an unwanted approach to my morning erection. I gasped, not out of pleasure. *Why the hell does she have such cold fingers?*

I pulled my hips back, withdrawing my package from her clutches, and slid out from under the covers. I walked over to the window, the sunlight prickling my naked skin, and pulled on a shirt and pair of slacks that were hanging off the back of a chair. Melany's bra lay strewn across the seat of the chair, her panties and skirt crumpled up on the ground next to it. She sat up in my bed and stared at me, holding the sheets up to cover her chest.

. . .

"I can arrange for a car to take you back to your hotel," I said, looking out the window. In the gardens down below, I saw my five-year-old nephew, Kota, sprinting around in his wolf form as my brother Christophe chased him. I smiled. His paws still seemed too big for his body and he was clumsy, but the little sprout was growing fast. Even after five years, it still was hard for me to believe my older brother was mated with a kid. Hell, it was hard to believe that *all* of my brothers were mated with kids. I was the last Luna standing. As the second eldest alpha, I wasn't used to having this kind of attention turned to me. The pressure had always been on Christophe, for being the eldest and the heir to our family name; and on Vander, because he was the sole omega of the family. There weren't many expectations placed on me, and unlike my youngest brother, Loch, I knew how to keep my parents satisfied.

Loch and I were similar in a lot of ways—at least before he'd gotten married. We had similar appetites for girls, though I may have been a little bit hungrier than him. We both had disdain for the rules of highborn life, but the difference was that I at least acknowledged the game and how to play it to my advantage. I'd been a diligent student. I followed our customs and, for the most part, kept my reputation clean. Most knew about my ways with women, and though I'm sure it wasn't approved of by a lot of the hoity-toity types in the highborn circle, I at least would never do anything dishonorable.

"Aren't you going to at least offer me breakfast?" Melany asked with a smile.

. . .

"I would, but I've got commitments." Breakfast was out of the question. Anything that would imply or encourage any emotional involvement was out of the question. And I did have a commitment.

"Oh," she said flatly, and slipped out of bed. I watched her move through the room, gathering her clothes, the morning sunlight hugging the curves of her naked body. She was beautiful, with the kind of slender frame that I liked. Last night, the thrill of seeing her naked would've given me a hard-on right away. Right now, I felt nothing. The thirst had been quenched. The want was gone.

"Would you like some coffee?" I asked. "I can have some ready for you in the car."

"That would be nice," she said, stepping into her clothes. "Help zip me up?"

I did, and then picked up the house phone on my desk and hit the number to dial Stephen, our head of staff. "Stephen, have a car readied for my guest, please? And have a cup of coffee waiting inside, too."

"I'll let you know the next time I'm in town?" she said as I walked her down to the front door. Stephen was waiting by the car, and he opened the back door for her.

. . .

I smiled and nodded. "I had a wonderful time with you last night," I said. I could see she wanted to kiss me, but she restrained herself and left a light peck on my cheek before getting into the car. Stephen shut the door behind her, and the driver pulled the car away. I watched until it had disappeared from sight down the long driveway out of the Luna estate.

I exhaled, and rolled up my sleeves. "Don't give me that look, Stephen," I said. I could see he was looking at me with a sliver of amusement. Of anyone in this house, Stephen knew my triumphs the best. Being the head of house staff, he'd helped me hide enough of them back in pre-academy when having a girl overnight at the house would've been a horrible offense. Now I was thirty-two. Having a woman over wasn't such a breach in family protocol, and Stephen had seen all the faces who'd come through.

"I don't have any idea what you mean, sir," he said, smiling.

"Sure, you don't. Do I have time for breakfast before the ceremony?"

"Of course. There's food waiting in the dining room."

A shrill howl of excitement pierced the air, and little Kota sprang around the front of the house, still in his wolf form. He sprinted at me as fast as he could and then jumped, shifting mid-air back into his little five-year-old human form. I caught him in my arms and lifted him up high.

"Woah there, kid."

Kota giggled, kicking his legs in the air. "Spin me around, Uncle Arthur!"

I did as I was told, and did a quick twirl on the ball of my foot with Kota held over my head. He laughed and squirmed, and I set him back on the ground. Christophe jogged around the corner, and Kota toddled over to him, wrapping an arm around his leg. My brother was only a year older than me, but it'd always felt like he outpaced me in maturity and grace by a decade. He'd grown up with the weight of responsibility on his shoulders, and two years ago he'd assumed his right as leader of our clan, the Crescent Moons, after our father abdicated.

It was a natural transition for Christophe. I knew he had some doubts about it, but it was obvious that leading was what he was meant to do. I'd graduated from the same school as him, the Dawn Academy's Alpha Leadership College, but I was far less suited for the work than him. I'd chosen the Leadership College simply because it sounded better than the other options. The healing arts were beyond my level of intelligence, and I wasn't cut out for the fighting arts. How could I be? I was a lover by nature.

. . .

"Good morning, Arthur," Christophe said, picking up his son under one arm. "Was I seeing things, or did you just whisk someone away into a car? Who was it this time?"

"Melany Dewall," I said plainly. "Do you remember her?"

"Of course. Rose Claw Clan. I had a clan meeting with her father last month. She's a smart girl. She'd be a good match, Arthur."

"Smart, but boring," I said. "And she has cold hands."

Kota squirmed out of Christophe's arms and shifted. He dropped to the ground in his wolf pup form and sprinted back towards the gardens.

"Hey!" Christophe called after him. "Don't get too worked up, Kota. You've got a Teller ceremony to attend to, remember?"

The little boy didn't seem to hear him, and bounced around in the grass and bushes, snapping at leaves with his jaws.

"Come on, Arthur. Isn't it time you met someone? Settled down?"

. . .

"I meet plenty," I said, smiling. "I haven't got any interest in settling down. What's the point? It's not for me, and I don't have any obligation to. The Luna brothers who need to settle are settled, and Mom and Dad are happy."

"Oh, I think they'd be a little happier to know all of their sons were mated," he said.

I laughed. "Is this what the head of the clan wants me to do?"

"No," he shrugged. "Just a brother looking out for his younger brother's happiness."

"Christophe. You don't think I'm happy? I'm living exactly the way I want to. You should know that."

"Feelings change. I mean look at *me*. A father, mated to the love of my life, and never been happier. You're telling me you don't want the family life? You could have this." He gestured over to where his boy was playing, and his expression changed as Kota did a circle around one of the rose bushes, lifted his hind leg, and peed. "KOTA!" Christophe shouted.

"I'm weeing, Dad!" Kota yelled back.

"I'm good," I told my brother, and patted him on the shoulder. "I'm going inside to grab some breakfast."

"The others should be here soon," he said.

"The Luna clan, all together again!"

With all of my brothers mated and living their own lives raising children, it'd become rare for us to all come together. In fact, it'd been a year since the last time the entire family had gathered. That time had been for Kota too, his first shift ceremony. Today we were taking him for his Teller ceremony, a tradition for a five-year-old where he would be blessed and have his future read by the clan shaman, or "Teller". I went back inside. Stephen was waiting at the entrance to the dining room, and he pulled open the door for me as I approached. Mom and Dad were seated at the long table, chatting over plates of breakfast.

"Good morning," I announced before diverting my attention to the buffet table. After filling my plate with a healthy portion of food I took a seat. My parents stopped their conversation and turned to me.

"Did you have someone over last night, Arthur?" Mom asked.

I looked up in surprise, swallowing down my mouthful of pork chop.

"I did," I said.

"And?" she said.

"And...?" I repeated. I wasn't used to having my parents, much less my mom, ask about the women I brought over. It wasn't exactly proper of me to be sleeping around so much, but given I did it discreetly and within the confines of the Luna estate, there'd always just been an unspoken understanding.

"How did it go?"

"It went fine, Mom," I said. "Everything's working as it should, thank you for asking."

"Anyone notable?" she asked. "The potential of something more?"

Dad looked at me with interest, waiting for my answer. I looked back and forth between them, feeling slightly perturbed by the sudden and unusual probing into my bed life. I cleared my throat. "No."

"You won't at least tell us who it was?"

. . .

"Out of respect for her privacy, no. Mom, you and I both know you can't keep anything to yourself."

"Oh," she said, "So, she's highborn, then?"

I sighed. "Yes. And nothing is gonna come of it. I'm not interested in a serious relationship, you should know that by now."

"It's going to become a problem," Dad said. "Bringing so many different women home, it's going to affect your reputation eventually. As prodigious as you are." He winked.

"Basch!" Mom shot him a look.

"I've already got a reputation, Dad. I wear it with pride."

"That's what I'm worried about," Mom said. "It's going to affect your chances at finding a mate. All your brothers are married, and you—"

"And I'm living my life exactly how I want to," I interrupted. "Marriage, children… It's not for everyone, and it's definitely not for me. We've gone over this." Mom and Dad exchanged another look. I was beginning to feel a little irritated. "My work with the clan is enough to keep me occupied. And my racing. Not to mention looking after you two old farts, now that everyone else has moved out."

"That's what the house staff is for," Mom protested. "You don't want to live the rest of your life alone, do you?"

"I'm not afraid of being alone, Mom. Besides, I'm highborn in one of the most powerful clans in Wolfheart. Time alone is a gift."

At that moment, the dining room doors opened and in flew my young niece Alexis, chasing after Kota. Behind the two children followed Christophe, his husband Mason, my youngest brother Vander, and his husband Pell. Mom scooped Alexis into her arms as Kota ran over to Dad and hid behind his chair.

"Let me down, Grandma!" Alexis squealed. "We're playing 'wolf and fox'! Kota's gonna get away."

"I'm the fox," Kota announced, and Dad picked him up and plonked him onto his lap.

"You're cheeky like a little fox, aren't you?" Dad said, pinching his cheek. I had to smile—Dad was a serious man, a grizzled old wolf worn down by the years as Crescent Moon leader. He only let this side of himself out around the grandkids.

. . .

"Grandpa, stop!" Kota laughed.

"I'm *starving!*" Vander said. "Good morning. Mom, Dad, hello."

He went around the table and gave hugs. Pell followed, hugging Mom and shaking Dad's and my hand.

"How's things at the clinic?" I asked Pell.

"Busy, as always. We're getting a lot more wolves coming into town now."

"You've gained weight," Mom said to Vander.

"It's all that bear food," Vander replied, laughing as he and Pell went to the buffet table to get breakfast. "It's delicious, and I swear we eat till bursting almost every night. Where's Loch and Tresten?"

"They just called," Christophe said. They'll be meeting us at the temple."

. . .

"Good morning," Mason said to me, pouring himself a cup of coffee.

"Not hungry?" I asked.

"Christophe and I already ate. We've been up for a few hours getting Kota ready."

"I'm going to give him a bath," Christophe said. "He decided to go rolling around in the grass."

"I don't need a bath," Kota protested.

"Yes, you do," Christophe said. "This is an important day for you, son. C'mon, let's go."

"Aww... I want to keep playing with Alexis. I want to show her the puzzle Aunt Jennifer gave me."

"You'll have plenty of time for that later. Let's go."

"Better listen to your father," Dad said, setting Kota back on the floor.

. . .

"So," Vander said, grinning at me. "How're things in the life of you? Still chasing tail?"

I groaned. "What the hell is with all the prying today?"

"I'll take that as a yes," Vander said, and everyone laughed.

It was nice having family back home. Admittedly, things could get a little quiet with just the three of us and the house staff in this gigantic complex that was our estate. I'd missed our family breakfasts, with all of my brothers here and Christophe fussing over us all, playing the family whip.

We ate breakfast and talked about our lives. Vander and Pell told us about the new healing clinics they were going to open in downtown Wolfheart, and Mason talked about the non-profit organization he'd recently started to offer assistance to lowborn neighborhoods. I updated them about my work with the clan, assisting Christophe with official duties and negotiations with other clans. It was challenging and necessary work, but not anything I enjoyed. I did it out of duty as the second eldest, not because it offered any kind of major enrichment to my life. What I *really* cared about was motorcycle racing—wolf-cycle racing, to be exact.

What was the difference? Speed and ferocity. A regular motorcycle could be raced with human response times, but a wolf-cycle required the reflexes of a shifted form. The rider rode immersed inside the vehicle, fore and hind legs stretched out as if in mid gallop. They were operated with delicate controls at each paw, and maxed out at a speed three times faster than regular human sport bikes. The racing courses were filled with treacherous obstacles that required split second reactions and heightened senses. There was nothing like the thrill of the race, not even chasing a new woman. My brothers were curious about my racing, but my parents were less than thrilled about it so I tried not to bring it up around them. Still, it'd been a long time since I'd seen them so it was hard not to get carried away when the conversation turned to bikes.

"You should've seen that race, Van," I said, my voice trembling slightly with excitement. "*Insanity*. Red Stallford and Vivian Elfang were leading the pack, I was right behind them. We hit four hundred miles an hour in the straightaway. The obstacles were coming at us like snow in a blizzard—so thick there wasn't a single inch for error. Red clipped his side on one of the pillars; thankfully it wasn't bad, but he was sent to the hospital with three broken legs. Vivian and I were muzzle to muzzle by the end. I remember everything was just a blur, I was so damn focused on that finish line. But, in the end, I was a better racer than her. Edged her out by one millisecond."

"I gotta admit, since becoming a healer, your racing became less thrilling and more nerve-wracking for me to hear about," Van said.

"Our team treated Red Stallford at the downtown clinic, actually," Pell said. "I saw the race. Hell of a finish, Arthur."

. . .

"Thank you, Pell. Someone who understands me."

"It was terrifying," Mom said. "And I can barely even keep track of what's going on, it's so fast. I die a little bit every time you race. I wish you'd give it up."

"Can't give up what I love most," I said.

"If only you'd divert that passion to a nice girl," she said. "Or boy. We know lots of eligible omegas."

"No, thanks," I said.

"You don't go for omegas, do you, Arthur?" Pell said. "Why not?"

"Not true," Christophe said, coming back into the room with Kota, who was all dressed up in his formal robe. "I remember when we were younger, in pre-academy, there was one. What was his name?"

I blinked. "Perichor," I said, a strange lump rising in my throat. "Perry."

. . .

"Perry. That's right."

Vander, Christophe, and Mom then began to argue about the most eligible highborn omegas in Wolfheart. Perry's name hung in the air like vapor, slowly dissipating after its momentary mention. Now I was recalling memories of Perry Houndfang, or when I knew him, Perry Windhelm. Funny that Perry be mentioned now—it was because of him that I'd discovered my passion for wolf-cycle racing. I'd immersed myself in it to escape the memory of him over a decade ago. I guess it'd worked. I hadn't thought of him in years. Funny how someone who meant so much could fade to the back of the mind. At one point in my life, he'd been all I wanted to think about. He'd been all I *wanted*. But he was gone from my life. Gone from this city. Gone for thirteen years.

Christophe's voice pulled me back to reality. "Arthur?"

I looked up. "Huh?"

"I asked, will you be taking the car with us to the ceremony, or…?"

"Oh. No, I'll take my motorcycle. I'll be going to the track afterwards."

"Well, we'd all better get going."

. . .

The wait staff came in to the dining room and started to clear the tables, and we all made our way towards the garage, where two cars were waiting, drivers standing at attention. Stephen came up and handed me my riding gear. The family piled into the cars, and I got onto my motorcycle and followed the caravan out of the garage. I drove alongside them for a while, waving at my niece and nephew, who made faces at me through the windows of the cars, before gunning the engine and taking off. Our family had access to a special, private highway reserved for highborn clans, and being completely empty of traffic except for our group, it was perfect for gaining some speed on. I roared ahead, zooming down into a subterranean tunnel that traveled directly into downtown Wolfheart. The orange tunnel lights flitted by in an increasing rhythm as I opened the throttle. The engine's cry rose to a fever pitch, and it felt like I was flying. This was speed—but it was human-limited speed. Later on, I'd climb into my wolf-cycle and get the real fix that I was craving.

I took an exit ramp that brought me out of the tunnel and into the city, and I was greeted by the insanity that was downtown Wolfheart. Just what I liked. I pulled off the private road onto the main one that led to the temple, threading around traffic like it was a wolf-cycle obstacle course. The temple appeared out of the concrete jungle like an enormous stone fang, a stark contrast of ancient architecture against modern skyscrapers. The entrance to the temple was flanked by two enormous stone statues of the legendary wolves who founded the city thousands of years ago. I swung my bike between them and entered the parking lot. I was early, of course.

. . .

After packing away my riding gear and putting on something a bit more formal, I made my way up to the entrance of the temple. The place used to creep me out as a kid. It was dingy and dark inside, lit with candlelight and thick with haze from all the incense being burned. The priests only made it worse—they walked around in half-human, half-wolf form, their gnarled old snouts protruding from beneath the darkened shroud of hooded cloaks.

I looked back over my shoulder when I heard the sound of a car rolling into the lot. I smiled—it was my brother Loch and his family.

"You're here early," I said, pulling him into a hug.

"Where's everyone else?" he asked.

"On their way. I took the bike."

"Ah, right. Should've guessed."

"Hello, Arthur," Tresten, his husband said to me, giving me a tight hug. Their ten-year-old son Ian hovered next to Tresten's side, his nose buried into a book.

"Hey, kid," I said, leaning over. Tresten nudged him.

. . .

"Ian? Your uncle is speaking to you."

"Hi, Uncle Arthur," he said, and gave me a quick hug before returning his focus to the book.

"Sorry," Tresten said. "We can hardly get him away from his books."

I shook my head. "No, that's great. He's passionate." I ruffled his hair, and he glanced up at me from the corner of his eye and smiled. I winked at him.

"Let's go inside?" Tresten suggested. "I'd like to make an offering in the temple before the ceremony."

As we walked into the temple, Loch told me about his position at the Dawn Academy's Fighting Arts School as an assistant master. "Can you imagine that? *Me*, as a teacher?"

"You're more than qualified," Tresten said. "Don't sell yourself short."

"Loch's got a point," I teased. "Would you really want a guy like him teaching students?"

. . .

Loch laughed. "Oh, young me probably would hate me as a teacher. I don't cut anyone any slack. I'm strict as hell."

"Really? Guess Dad rubbed off on you after all. You must be happy, Tresten, to have your husband working alongside you."

We entered the main hallway of the temple, lit by rows of hundreds of candles. Ian finally emerged from his book, sticking close to Tresten's leg, his eyes wide as they looked around the cavernous space. Tendrils of incense curled from golden wolf skulls, and the priests shuffled around paying little attention to us, murmuring prayers to themselves.

"Actually," Tresten said, "the reason why Loch was asked to teach is because I'm going to be taking a leave of absence." We turned a corner towards an alcove where several shrines were held; three small trees growing out from the stone, with chains of gold hanging from their branches—the shrines for omega fertility and healthy childbirth. Tresten shifted into his wolf form, stepped up to the trees, and lowered his nose to the bark in tribute. I connected the dots.

"Hounds of Hell. Tresten, you're pregnant again?"

Loch grinned proudly. "We're having another kid,"

"Guys, that's fantastic! Congratulations to the both of you."

. . .

"It was completely unexpected," Tresten said. "But a welcome surprise."

We walked back towards the entrance to the temple to meet the rest of the family that would be arriving at any moment.

"Another kid," I said to my brother. "Loch Luna, family man and Dawn Academy master. Never could've seen that coming ten years ago."

"Hey, I was always an awesome fighter. Just not the most disciplined student."

"Things change, I guess."

He smiled. "You haven't changed much, Arthur. From what I've heard, you're still up to no good. Breaking hearts. You sure you don't want to settle down?"

"Ah, Hounds of Hell. Not you, too. Everyone's on my ass today about my damn love life."

"Really?"

. . .

"Yeah. I'm not interested in that shit, you know that. Mom started even started suggesting omegas… No offense, Tresten."

"What's wrong with omegas?" he asked.

"Nothing," I said.

"Nothing," Loch said, "except he won't date them. You had a bad experience with an omega, didn't you? That old thing from when we were in pre-academy. You know he's back, right?"

I hadn't expected to hear those words, and my heart jumped so hard it was in danger of bursting out of my throat. I coughed. "Who told you that?" I said, trying to sound unaffected.

"His younger brother studies at the Academy. Overheard it."

At that moment, the rest of the family entered the temple, and Loch, Tresten, and Ian went to go greet them. What had been just a bit of throwaway information to Loch had completely rocked me. I was stewing in my thoughts as my body ran on autopilot, moving my legs to follow the group as we moved to the room where Kota's ceremony would take place. Everything around me seemed to be moving in blurs and echoes.

. . .

It was like a hole had been torn into the wall I'd set up in my mind, and all the thoughts and feelings I'd blocked away were gushing out of it. My heart was pounding. I was in shock. How could those words affect me like this? I'd gotten over all of this a long time ago. I'd gotten over *him* a long time ago. But I'd believed that I would never see Perry again. We promised each other that we would break contact forever. He was married. He lived far away. I'd never see him again, never have to think about him again.

But now, apparently Perry was back in Wolfheart.

Of course, I was sure he came back occasionally to visit, but I'd never known about it. I'd remained in blissful ignorance for these past years, believing that I'd never have to think about him again. Now, suddenly, his presence was back in my mind, like an ember rekindled.

I stood in the darkness of the Teller's chambers as Christophe walked his son towards the blind old priest. A thick haze of incense and candle smoke surrounded me, and I found myself falling into my memories, drifting back in time thirteen years to the time when Perry Windhelm was still in my life, and when I was in love with an omega.

PERRY

"regor doesn't know you're here?"

Dad paced back and forth, his eyes trained on the carpet. Jupiter played quietly next to my chair, distracted with a little toy wolf. She was three, and had grown adept at tuning out the arguments and serious conversations of adults. Our life back in Elclaw, with her father, Gregor, made that an easy task.

"No," I said. "I just took Jupiter and left. I'd had enough."

"Oh," Dad said, pushing his gray hair back. I could see what was going through his head—he was trying to think up of a way to make this "right," to apologize to Gregor and send me and my daughter back to Elclaw. Dad was just like that. He wasn't a bad person in any sense, but his mind was always on

26

the status of our family name and whether or not it was in "appropriate standing" or not. Our family got prestige from being married in to the Houndfangs and their Silver Sun Clan, so me walking out on my cheating bastard of a husband was a problem for Dad.

"It's not too late to make all this right," Dad continued. He was just talking to himself at this point, giving himself reassurances. "Yes. You can call home and say that… that I was sick. You came home to visit me."

"Hounds of Hell, Dad. Are you serious?"

"Of course I'm serious, Perichor. And you should be too. This is your family's name you're dealing with. If word gets around that you've walked out, that you two are having problems… The gossip will be extraordinary, and I don't know what I'll be able to do for you then."

"I don't give a damn about any gossip. I'm not going back, Dad. Not to a man who's been bringing women *and* omegas into our bedroom for years. I never wanted this marriage, but I gave it a fair shot. He had so many chances, and blew every single one of them. Force me out of the house, or out of the family if you want. I'm not going back."

Dad looked hurt. He leaned against the couch and rubbed his forehead. "I know the situation is less than desirable, Perichor... But we're highborn. You and Gregor are bound under the seal of the high wolf clans. You can't just leave. You have to go back."

"The longer I stay there with him, the faster my soul deteriorates. I'll have nothing left. I'm withering away, Dad. And our daughter, she'll be affected too. She already is."

It wasn't just the infidelity. Gregor could be an angry, hateful man, especially when it came to interrupting his lifestyle. He'd never lifted a hand against me or Jupiter, but he struck with his words and voice. The shouting matches were so frequent and intense that many of our house staff had quit. I wish I could say that he was at least a good father, but he hardly had a care to participate in our daughter's life. The Houndfangs were the wealthiest family in Elclaw, and Gregor basked in that lifestyle. Extravagant parties. Competitive wolf-cycle racing. Traveling for "business". And of course, all the temptation that came with those things.

I guess I had to say that the cheating didn't bother me so much. I might've thought I'd loved him for a brief period when Jupiter was born, but now there was nothing. It was the disrespect, and the example he was setting for our daughter. The irresponsibility, the lack of character. And I was bitter that I'd been forced to sacrifice my life in Wolfheart to be with him, to waste so many years of my youth suffering. There were times when I wished he would change, and that maybe at least we could have a calm life together. I didn't need to love him, but at least we could have that. Of course, that wasn't possible. That wasn't who he was. But more than anything, I wished I could just be done with him.

"You're here now," Dad said, his expression softening. "So what else can we do? You and Jupiter will stay here for as long as possible. But eventually, you will have to go back. I'm sorry, son. I wish there was something we could do, but you and Jupiter will be better off there than living in exile. I know you know this. So please, think about that."

He was right. That was the worst part of it.

The door to the living room opened and my brother Dimitrius came in, towel draped around his neck. He was a first year at the Dawn Academy's Fighting Arts School, and must've just gotten back from classes.

"Hey," he said to us, and then crouched down next to Jupiter. "How's my niece doing, huh? You having fun, there?"

Jupiter looked up at him, smiled, and continued to play with her wolf. She was a quiet girl and didn't like to talk much to other people, except me.

"Everything good, Perry?" Dimitrius asked.

. . .

I smiled, not wanting to burden my brother. "Everything's fine."

"You sure? You want me to beat Gregor up for you? Because I will." He threw out several rapid jabs and a kick.

"I'm pretty sure the FAS wouldn't appreciate that type of behavior from one of their students," I said. "But thanks. I wish it were that easy."

"If you want me to babysit Jupiter for you, just let me know. It's been a while since you've been back home. You should have some time to check the city out."

"I'm not really here for sightseeing, Dimitrius."

"I know. But you've been through a lot. You should have some time to yourself. Right, Dad?"

"Uh, sure. Of course."

Dimitrius rolled his eyes. I knew he didn't respect our father.

"Go," he urged. "I know you want to get out and check things out. It's alright."

. . .

"Fine, fine," I said. He was right, anyway. Waiting around at home would just drive me crazy. I was in limbo here.

I went upstairs to my old bedroom, which had long ago been converted into a study, and changed my clothes from my suitcase. Next to it was Jupiter's miniature pink suitcase. I felt terrible. I wished I didn't have to be here. I wished I didn't have to run. I hated that Jupiter had to be put through all this, and I hated that my father wasn't more helpful. I knew he was right, his hands were tied, but I wished he could've at least been more supportive and understanding. If Mom were still alive, it would've been the same way. She'd been the one to set up the damn arrangement with the Houndfangs, and all because she felt our family was "too poor." Not enough status, not enough money.

It was the first time I was back in Wolfheart on my own in over ten years. Where would I go? One place immediately came to mind.

The White Tree Wolf-Cycle Track brought me mixed feelings. Watching the races had been a great passion when I was younger, but my love for the sport had been tainted because of my husband's participation in it. Still, it was where I ended up going, almost automatically.

It was open race day, with amateurs and semi-pros taking to the track to practice their runs. The huge stadium was only half-filled, but still bursting with excited energy. It'd been ages since I'd been to a race, and my heart immediately began to pound as the familiar smell of gasoline hit my nose, followed by the ghoulish whine of wolf-bike engines. It was impossible not to get swept up in the atmosphere, in the excitement of it all. It didn't hurt that White Tree was the largest, the most complicated, and the most dangerous track in the world.

When I was just getting to know Gregor, I'd clung to his aptitude for bike racing as the one possible saving grace, the one piece of connection that I thought we might've been able to share. He'd ruined that too.

With plenty of seats available I was able to find a good position overlooking the track, with clear views of the major obstacles. There was the Dog's Eye, a series of narrow vertical loops rising a hundred feet in the air; The Walls, a section of parallel walls that required a high level of speed to maintain traction; and the most dangerous, The Forest—a section after the final straightaway filled with scattered concrete pylons that the riders needed to weave around at breakneck speed.

I'd arrived in the middle of a race. Different views of the tracker were projected onto giant screens hanging above the stands, overlaid with information about the different competitors. The crowd roared as the bikes exploded past the stands into the first straightaway of the final lap. Two were neck and neck, with another two not far behind.

. . .

Hounds of Hell, they're fast.

Having not seen a race in so long, I'd forgotten what it was like to see such speed. It was invigorating, like nothing else. They seemed to be constantly on the verge of being out of control, like they could pull apart or collide into the obstacles at any moment, and every time they seemed just on the edge of disaster, they avoided it. And the sound! The sound of the bikes was like the shrill howl of a banshee wolf, underlined with a deep pulsing vibrato that shook your very core.

It'd been such a long time, but I was remembering everything. I was actually enjoying myself, for once.

The two leaders zipped into the Dog's Eye, skirting the narrow loops with dizzying precision. The crowd gasped—me included—when one of the tail bikes lost the path and shot off loop, launching into the air like a missile. It soared high and then exploded as the inner control pod jettisoned from the main body and floated back down to the ground with the aid of two parachutes. Smoke drifted from the downed pod as rescue teams rushed out to aid the driver.

The leaders exited the Dog's Eye unscathed, pushing into a series of hairpin turns that crisscrossed up a steep hill. I was on the edge of my seat now, my pulse racing as fast as the wolf-cycles on the track. The first bike carved ahead, pulling away just slightly from the second rider. An *"oooh"* rose up from the crowd. The bikes hurtled onto ramps that split the trick into a Y fork, curving upward so that they were vertical. It was The Walls. They pushed their speed to maintain their climb and ride. The second bike faltered a bit, and for a second it looked as if he was going to lose that critical level of speed needed to keep the bike stuck on the wall, but suddenly, just at the last minute, he corrected. The third bike didn't miss his chance to take advantage of the mistake. He zipped around number two, taking second place. This guy was *good*! I realized I was biting my lip out of nervous excitement, a habit I'd forgotten I once had.

They were out of The Walls and into the final straightaway. I rose to my feet along with the rest of the crowd—the most dangerous section was just ahead. The new second bike managed to close the distance between him and the leader, bringing them neck and neck. I found myself rooting for this guy, whoever he was. He was a clear underdog, and a damn good rider. His bike shot forward like a steel blue laser next to the leader's crimson streak. The straightaway opened up into a field of a thick, concrete pylons that increased in number as they neared the finish line. Many of the pylons were charred and blackened from crashes. The riders split away from each other, each looking for their own path through The Forest. There was no room to slow down. Any decrease in speed to avoid a pylon would inevitably mean a loss— or a crash. This was on the edge riding at its most intense.

The red bike zipped a line through the pylons, avoiding them with exact precision. Blue was the same. They were on opposite sides of the field, but it was easy to see they were still neck and neck. The finish line was closing in fast. Would the victory come down to inches?

The crowd was silent in anticipation now, the stadium filled only with the whine of the engines. Blue had a slight advantage... Or was it red? It was impossible to tell.

I cringed as blue came close to clipping a pylon, swerving around it, its back tire giving off a puff of white smoke. *Shit.* Had he just screwed himself over?

Wait...

Blue was taking what seemed to be a clear path through the pylons, the best way to go at what seemed like the fastest speed—until he *increased* his speed. They were taking their bike mere inches away from each pylon, hardly turning to avoid them. I felt goosebumps prickle my skin as my heart skipped a beat. I'd seen this driving before. No, more than that, I'd been intimate with this technique. I'd only known one driver who'd made it their signature.

"Fuck yeah!" someone shouted. "Go, Luna!"

My mouth dropped open. *No way.* Could it really be him? But did I really need to ask that? Who else could it be? Who else was named Luna who drove like that in The Forest on the final lap of the race? I'd only known one.

. . .

Arthur Luna.

My legs felt weak, and my body tingled with excitement, but this time it wasn't from the race. I hadn't thought about Arthur for years. I hadn't even heard his name in years.

I was still in disbelief that blue bike down there could really belong to Arthur Luna, but there really was no one else it could be. The Lunas were a prominent family in Wolfheart. Not just anyone had that last name, and Arthur had been the only one of his four brothers to race wolf-cycles.

The crowd around me erupted into a roar. He'd won the race, but I was barely even paying attention anymore. I stood transfixed, watching as the blue bike curved around the track. All I wanted to see was who would emerge from the bike, but because it was just an open race day and not an official event, the bike drove along to the pit and disappeared into the underground bays. A new set of bikes immediately rode out, and the next races began. Someone behind me cleared their throat, and I realized that the rest of the crowd had resumed their seats, leaving me the only one standing like an idiot. I quickly sat down, my heart still pounding in my chest.

How strange was it that someone who'd once been so important to me had all but completely left my mind? Maybe it'd been the trauma of our separation that'd forced me to sacrifice my memories of him. If I traced things back, that time had been the start of this life I was now living...

Arthur and I had met in pre-academy, at the Delson Preparatory School for Young Wolves. We spent three years together there—two years and eleven months as the closest friends, and one month as something much more.

I got up from my seat and left the stands, going down into the auditorium where I knew of a secret maintenance route that would take me down into the bike staging area. I needed to see if it really was him.

The marriage to Gregor Houndfang had been arranged years before Arthur and I had met. I'd never had a say in the matter, nor had I really questioned or objected to it. I'd grown up knowing that I would marry into the Houndfang family, believing that it was for the good of my family. I'd gone through most of my young life committed to that duty, not concerned about love—I was already engaged, and I believed I would never fall in love with anyone, anyway.

I found the maintenance route and slipped down it. I straightened my shirt and walked with purpose, passing by a group of mechanics who didn't even give me a second glance. My pulse was racing now, soaring as fast as the pulse of pistons in a wolf-cycle's engine. I felt almost dizzy with excitement. What would I do if it was him? What would I say? So many things were rushing through my mind.

. . .

Would he want to see me? Would he be happy to see my face again?

His face... Even though it'd been so many years, I could still picture him in my mind perfectly.

Long forgotten feelings were starting to bubble up as the memories of our time together returned to me, and longing cinched tightly around my heart. It hurt. I remembered how close we used to be, how Arthur had been the first person in my life I'd felt truly understood me. No, the *only* person. I'd never known you could feel such comfort to be around another person until I'd met him. Everything was coming back to me now as I rushed down that hallway.

I pushed through the doors marked "Authorized Access Only" and emerged in the bike staging area. Crews worked on bikes, filling the air with the echoing sound of ratchet guns and tuning rods and the pungent smell of gasoline and hot rubber. I made my way down the rows of bikes and their crews, looking for that bike, the blue one, and the face of the wolf who was emerging from the depths of my memories.

I remembered when he'd confessed his feelings to me. It was a month before our graduation. A month before I was to leave for Elclaw. A month before I was going to be married. I remembered the confusion and anguish I'd felt—if only he'd told me sooner, if only we'd had more time together, if only my family had been in a better position, if only I didn't have to be married to a man I didn't love. I'd fallen for my best friend. I loved Arthur. I'd pushed him so completely out of my memories because of *this* feeling. This aching. It'd hurt too damn much leaving him. It'd been like a deep and agonizing wound, and the mind does what it can to prune away memories too painful to live with.

I froze in my tracks when I saw the blue bike ahead. It'd just pulled into its space, shimmering waves of heat still rippling from its cobalt surface. Three pit crew members approached it, spraying it with water to cool its surface. There was a hiss as the compartment door latch released and pushed open, and the door swung around to the top of the bike, revealing the inner cockpit. Then I saw him. He stepped out, his black fur shimmering with droplets of water caught from the spray, and he shook them off before shifting back to human form. My heart caught in my throat as his fur pulled back to skin and his paws became hands and feet. His muzzle shrunk, and his wolf visage turned to the handsome features of the man from my memories.

Hounds of Hell, he looked good. Time had brought ruggedness to his features, a hard maturity he didn't have before.

My curiosity was confirmed, and I should've just nipped it in the bud right there. Going any further from here would be a mistake. Nothing good could come out of it. But controlling impulses was never a strength of mine. If it had been, Arthur and I never would've become lovers in the first place.

. . .

Two women approached him excitedly—apparently, I wasn't the only one who knew how to access this place—and they talked to him with stars in their eyes. I picked up my courage and strode forward. The way he spoke to the women, I could see he was used to this kind of attention. That shouldn't have been surprising given his status, his looks, and the fact that he had become a very skilled rider, but I remembered how shy he used to be when I knew him. Obviously, time had brought changes for the both of us.

He caught me approaching out of the corner of his eye and turned to greet me with a cordial smile on his face, like he was greeting another fan. I saw the flash of recognition in his eyes, and he took a step backwards like he'd been punched in the gut. The smile disappeared and was replaced by a look of shock. We stood, just staring at each other. The women continued to try and speak to him, but he wasn't listening. They looked back and forth between us, and then left, looking annoyed.

"Hi, Arthur," I said. "Long time no see."

"Perry...?"

Despite all the aching memories that had resurfaced, I had to smile. I was happy to see him. Really happy.

"Hounds of Hell. It's really you," he said. It sounded like he was talking to himself, like he was convincing himself that this was real. I understood. It didn't feel real. Thirteen years, and I'd never thought I'd see him again. But here he was. Here *we* were.

"It's me," I said, matter-of-factly. I realized I was trembling. He stared at me, and I thought I saw a flash of pain in his eyes.

"What are you doing here?" he asked. "How'd you know I would be here?"

"I just came to see the track. I didn't know you'd be here. You raced well out there. You've improved a lot since I last saw you."

Finally, his expression softened. A slight smile crept across his lips. "I've had a long time to practice."

"This is your bike?" I said, gesturing to it. "GX57 'Howl'. You always liked the aggressive styles."

Next to a man, a wolf-cycle stood almost head height, its body about as long as a mid-sized car. It had a stretched, jet-like cockpit window and a tapered end. Arthur's bike was angular, with sharp edges for aerodynamics. Looking at it, it gave the impression of a wolf leaping at its prey. Arthur laid his hand against its side.

. . .

"You still know your shit," he said, looking impressed. "I've been driving this one for the past four years. Killer performance. Amazing responsiveness."

"I heard they really worked out the kinks in the 56 model," I said. "What a delicious piece of machinery." I went over to it and peered into the ventilation gap along the side that revealed a portion of the engine. Arthur leaned in too, his face close to mine. He pointed at the reflex valves running along the side of the engine.

"Damn right, they did. Increased shift synchronicity and a higher fuel flow-off. Three hundred fifty times."

"Incredible. No wonder you were able to pull off such precise maneuvers. I knew it was you when I saw how you tackled The Forest. I recognized that driving right away."

"Mm."

We both seemed to become aware of our proximity to one another at that moment, and moved away. Silence passed between us again, broken only by the sounds of the garage. He eyed me, and I felt my heart flutter nervously. I knew what was on his mind.

"What are you doing back here? In Wolfheart, I mean," he asked quietly. "I never thought I'd see you again."

. . .

"It's not a story to tell in a place like this," I said. "It's complicated."

"Well, perhaps we should go somewhere where you can tell me."

Suddenly, I was hesitant. Coming here was probably a mistake. Seeing him was a mistake.

"That might not be the best idea," I said.

"Why? Ah. Because your husband wouldn't like it, right? Where is the guy?"

"No," I said, with a flash of anger. "He's not here."

"Oh."

Arthur gave me an intrigued look. I sighed.

"I told you, it's complicated."

"And it's been thirteen years since I've seen you."

. . .

I knew what I was getting myself into, coming down here to find him. It might've been a mistake, but it was a mistake I'd made willingly. And despite better judgement, I did want to tell him everything. I could've made it easy for the both of us and walked away at that moment. It would've been cruel to show up like this and then disappear again without a word, but in the long run doing that would be the wise decision. But I wasn't making wise decisions.

After thinking for a moment, I asked, "Do you remember where our spot is?"

"Yes. Of course."

"Then meet me there. One hour."

"Fine."

"Okay." I looked at him, taking all of him in. I wondered what he'd gone through these past years. Had he suffered like me? Or had he gotten along? I turned to leave.

"Hey," he said, and I paused. "You aren't going to disappear, are you?"

. . .

"I'll be there," I said. "Our spot. One hour." And then I turned and left, not looking back.

Arthur Luna, back in my life. This was not the turn of events I'd been expecting.

ARTHUR

My motorcycle trembled between my legs as I cranked the throttle and tore out of Wolfheart and into the forest-covered mountains that surrounded the city. I felt like I was barely holding on. My mind was twisting, everything churning around like it was caught in a storm of confused emotion. Perry had just walked back into my life, as naturally as if he hadn't been gone for thirteen years.

What the hell was he doing, coming and seeing me after all this time?

Memories flashed through my head, ones that I'd fought to forget. Memories of days spent in each other's arms, convincing myself that everything would somehow work out in our favor, and love would win, and Perry wouldn't actually have to leave Wolfheart to get married to a man who wasn't me. I was young and naïve then. Just a dumb kid who'd fallen head over paws in love with his best friend.

Why'd he have to come and find me?

Shit. Why the hell was I crying?

I flipped up the visor of my helmet to let the wind dry the few tears that collected at the corners of my eyes, and pulled my bike off the highway and into the trees past a rusted sign that read "Golden Forest Proving Grounds." Our spot.

The old racetrack was once where all the wolf-cycle races in Wolfheart were held, but was closed several decades ago when the White Tree Clan sponsored the construction of a new track to be built in the heart of the city, using new standards and obstacles which brought Wolfheart into the competitive circuit. Until that time, Elclaw had been the capital of wolf-cycle racing, and all the best riders were from there. My bike had been designed there. Even though the Golden Forest track was no longer used for competition and was technically closed to the public, riders continued to bring their bikes there to practice for the real deal. Perry and I'd used to go there all the time. I would do practice runs, he'd give me feedback and help tune the bike, and we'd spend hours just sitting up on top of the old commentator's box, watching other racers run the old track.

. . .

It was also the only place we could go to get away from the reality of our situation—we were in a love that wasn't meant to be. We could be together there, away from the prying eyes of Perry's parents.

I hadn't been back to the Golden Forest Proving Grounds since the day he'd left me. In a way, maybe that was what'd rocketed me forward as a racer. I'd been forced to spend my time at the White Tree track, riding alongside the pros and tackling a true wolf-cycle obstacle course.

It was already approaching early evening and the grounds were quiet. The rumble of my bike's engine echoed across the abandoned lot as I pulled in, kicking up a flutter of fallen leaves in my wake. There was a single car parked in the middle of the gigantic lot, and I left my bike next to it. Without the stadium lights to illuminate the track, the place felt lonely and vast. The looming obstacles of the course were silhouetted against the pale evening sky, dark shapes like the geometry of an abstract painting. Up at the announcer's box, I saw the sweep of a flashlight floating around like a firefly. I took a breath, straightened my shirt, and started the climb up the many stairs towards the box.

This was crazy. Meeting Perry here again was crazy. Maybe I'd gone crazy.

But no, as I climbed up the rusted access ladder and pulled myself onto the roof of the announcer's box, he really was there. He sat on the edge looking out over the race track, his legs dangling over the side. The wind rustled his hair, carrying a swirl of leaves up from the ground into a vortex around him. As if sensing my presence, he looked back over his shoulder at me, brushing his blonde hair back from his forehead. In the fading light, he almost didn't look real. Like he was a spirit, or something.

"Tell me what the hell is going on," I said, not moving any closer. Everything I'd locked away was there, I could feel it smoldering on the edge of my mind, threatening to break free again, and I was afraid to get pulled back into the madness that was being so in love with someone who loved you back, but could never really be with you.

"I ran," he said, his voice steady and clear.

"Why?"

"Because my husband is a cheating, manipulative, horrible pile of dog shit. Everything you knew he'd be. I couldn't stand to have him near my little girl any longer."

Little girl. Perry had a daughter.

"So I ran back to Wolfheart," he went on. "I'd tried before, but he'd stopped me. Guilted me, threatened me, convinced me not to. Finally, I'd had enough and just left. I took Jupiter and came back. So, here I am. Here for now. Until my dog shit husband comes around to 'claim his omega' and haul Jupiter and me back to Elclaw."

Perry's expression was steeled and calm, but I could hear the emotion burning in his voice.

"Hounds of Hell," I muttered. It hurt to hear this from him. I'd wanted to believe that all this time, Perry had been living happily in Elclaw and that my intuition about his then fiancé had been off the mark. Thirteen years. He'd been going through this for that long? I felt a flame of anger flickering up in my heart, both because he'd been hurt and because I hadn't been able to do anything to help him. I was a Luna, a member of the Crescent Moon Clan, one of the most powerful in Wolfheart—and it hadn't meant anything.

I went to him and without hesitation, wrapped my arms around him. I could feel him trembling softly as he relaxed against my body. I hugged him tighter, silently willing his pain away. "I'm sorry, Perry," I said, and I felt his arms slowly wrap around me. His warm and familiar scent instantly transported me back in time. I felt like I was thirteen years younger. I closed my eyes.

"Fate is either kind or cruel," he said, "for bringing me back to you."

We sat down next to each other on the ledge of the announcer's box and stared out across the race track.

. . .

"I can't believe you're actually here," I said. "It doesn't feel real."

"I know," he said, and sighed. "I hope you won't be upset to hear that I hadn't intended to come to Wolfheart to find you. It really was an act of fate. I'm not here with the expectation of anything from you. It just so happened that I went to the White Tree stadium while you were racing."

"I'm not upset," I said. "Can I be honest with you?"

"You know you can."

"I'd almost forgotten you existed."

He looked at me, but I saw no offense in his eyes. "Because anything else would've been too painful. I understand. I had to force myself to forget, too, in order for me to live a normal life." Perry looked away and rubbed his hands anxiously in his lap.

"So... What are you going to do?" I asked.

He shook his head. "I have no idea. My dad has been unhelpful. He's as spineless as ever."

. . .

"I'm guessing your mom isn't on your side either, huh?"

"Well," he said, "No. She died four years ago."

"Oh," I said in a tone of surprise that might've sounded a bit too pleasant. "Sorry," I added.

Perry smiled. "The world's better off without her. Especially me and my brother."

"Dimitrius," I said, "My brother told me he's studying at the Fighting Arts School."

"A first year. He's all fired up to become a master fighter," Perry said.

"He was just a little kid the few times I met him. So… you have a kid, huh?"

"That's right," Perry said, a bright smile spreading across his lips. It was like his entire aura changed at that moment, and I saw a glimpse of a Perry that I *had* forgotten. "Jupiter. She's my light, and the one single good thing that's come from Gregor."

. . .

"How old is she?"

"She's three and a half."

"She must be wonderful."

He nodded. "She is. She's a treasure." Then that spark in his eyes faded, and I could see the conflict stirring there like a churning grey sea. A thought came to my mind that boiled my anger.

"Perry, he's not harming you or Jupiter, is he? Has he raised a hand to you?"

"No," he said. "He'd never do that. He's not that much of a monster, thankfully. Just a man with total disregard for anyone but himself."

"Alright," I said. I didn't know what I would've done if his answer had been different.

"I'm going to have to go back to him," Perry said. "After all this, Jupiter and I will end up back there. I can deal with it, but I'm afraid for my daughter. She's already growing up in such a terrible environment. The arguing is one thing, but there's the gambling, the drinking, the whoring... He's a wolf-cycle racer too, actually." His smile was sad now. "I never in a million years would've thought I'd come to feel distaste for the sport, but... I hardly ever watch it these days. Yours was the first race I'd seen in years."

"Hounds of Hell," I muttered. "This all feels so familiar. It's like... reliving those last few weeks we spent together before you were swept away."

"I'm sorry," he said, placing his hand on the back of mine. "I hate that I'm unloading all of this onto you, Arthur." I felt a chill run up my arm, a shiver of excitement that had long been absent from my life. All the women I'd brought into my bed, and none of them could cause that reaction in me. "Being here with you like this, seeing you again... I feel comfortable. This is the first time I've felt this comfortable in years. Isn't that weird?"

"No," I said. "I know exactly what you mean."

The last glimmer of sunlight cast deep purple hues across the sky. My heart ached as I remembered everything we'd shared, and all the memories I'd suppressed were fully released. It felt like I was remembering a whole 'nother life that I'd lived. I guess it was. I was a different person then, and the man next to me was at the center of it. Amazing, how a month could feel like a lifetime, and yet not enough time when spent with someone you cared about so much.

. . .

"I've really missed you, Perry," I said. It wasn't so much a declaration as it was a realization, and I was surprised to hear the words as they escaped my mouth. "I didn't even know how much."

"Me too, Arthur," he said. I looked at him, and in the dusk light his eyes seemed as deep as the sea. He gazed back at me.

Then, we were back thirteen years ago. Right here. This spot. Our first kiss. The first time we made love. Our goodbyes.

His hand snuck into mine, and our fingers intertwined. I leaned in, and he met me with his lips. His kiss sent lightning through me, waking up parts of my soul that I hadn't even realized had gone dormant. I'd shut him out of my memories for thirteen years, along with *this* feeling. Hounds of Hell, I'd forgotten what it felt like. *Love*. I still loved him. It'd been there, locked away all this time, unavailable to anyone else except for the one man who had the key.

I slipped my hand around the back of his neck, drawing him closer to me. Our tongues met, teased and intertwined. I felt a life surge between my thighs that I hadn't even realized I'd been missing.

"Damn," I whispered.

. . .

"I think I'd forgotten how good a kiss could feel," Perry murmured.

I wrapped my arm around his shoulder and he rested his head on mine.

What was *I* going to do? After Perry had left Wolfheart, I'd spent so much time tearing myself up over what I could've done or should've done to help him, but in the end, none of it mattered because he was gone and I couldn't change the past. Suddenly, unexpectedly, I had another chance.

But what could I really do?

And did I really want to get involved? I wasn't the same person that I was back then. I'd gone my own path, just like Perry had gone his. I couldn't chase a memory of what we had.

"It's getting late," Perry said. He stood up, and my hand slid away from his shoulder. "I should be getting home. My daughter is waiting for me."

"You're at your family estate?" I asked.

"Yeah."

. . .

We climbed down from the roof of the building and made our way down the stadium stairs to the debris-covered tarmac. Grass and weeds were starting to poke through cracks in the asphalt, and birds hopped around picking at bugs in the overgrowth. Give another ten years, and our spot would probably be unrecognizable. As we walked out towards the parking lot, our hands hung by our sides, just a few inches apart. I wanted to reach out and take his hand, but I resisted. I wasn't used to this nervous feeling. It was like I was eighteen again, full of butterflies.

I swung my leg over the seat of my motorcycle, my helmet squeezed underneath my arm.

"You don't need to worry about me, Arthur," Perry said, standing by the door to his car. "In fact, I'm sorry to have gotten you involved again. I didn't expect that we'd be seeing each other again, like this. So I think it's probably for the best we let things be."

Before it goes any further. I knew that was what he meant. But I'd tasted him again, and felt the warmth of his touch. The den had been opened.

"It's too late, Perry," I said. "For better or for worse, we've been thrown back into each other's lives. We're gonna see each other again. I'm gonna take care of you."

. . .

I twisted the key in the ignition and my bike growled to life, its throaty roar cutting the quiet of this place. The way Perry looked at me, I could see that he wasn't surprised at my response. He knew as well as I did that there was nothing either of us could do. We were together again. There was no going back, no ignoring it. I slipped on my helmet. Jamming my boot onto the pavement, I opened the throttle and swung my back tire around, burning rubber and kicking up an arc of pale smoke. Then I released the brake and rocketed away.

Life didn't often give second chances. I wasn't going to waste this one.

* * *

I slugged back a whiskey and ordered one more. Loch sat next to me, turning his glass on the counter. The lounge musician played something unremarkable on the piano as people feigned interest to get away from their conversations for a moment.

"And he just showed up out of nowhere?" Loch said.

"Yeah," I said. "Appeared like a fucking ghost."

"What are the odds," he said. "Just after I told you I learned he was back. You don't think he's trying…" He stopped himself, considering his words. "Do you trust him?"

. . .

"Yes," I said, without hesitation. "I know how it looks. Convenient appearance after thirteen years, needing help. Perry isn't like that. And he's not asking for anything from me."

"Okay," Loch said. "Sorry. Didn't mean to cause any offense."

I shook my head. "It's a fair assumption." I sipped more whiskey. I probably shouldn't drink this much, but I was trying to make sense of this whole situation.

"I didn't realize he meant this much to you," Loch said. "You never talked about him much."

"I couldn't," I said, swirling the drink in my glass. "It was just too much." I sighed. "I'm not used to feeling out of control, Loch. It feels the way I did back then. Out of control. I need to help him, but I don't know what I can do. He's bound to this marriage. It's a bond that can't be broken."

"The sacred oath isn't easily broken, that's for sure," Loch said, nodding.

"It's a good thing you and Tresten worked out, huh? You would've been in the same situation."

. . .

He chuckled. "Don't remind me. I understand what Perry must be going through. It can only be worse as omega, though. To have your life signed away like that, bound to an alpha you don't love. Damn. Poor Tresten. He got stuck with me."

We both laughed. "It really is amazing that it did work out," I said. "Fortunate."

"Fate worked in our favor," Loch said. "I've learned to trust in fate. When it blows good stuff your way, you gotta take it. And you know, I think it's blowing your way. There's gotta be some way to dissolve their marriage."

"Yeah," I said, not sounding so sure. The sacred laws of mating and marriage went back thousands of years. Omegas and betas belonged to their alpha. Once the rites were performed, the bond was solid in the eyes of society—especially for highborns. Omegas and betas risked being ostracized from their families and clans if they tried to separate from their mates.

"I work at the Dawn Academy," Loch said. "I'll ask some of my friends there to look into the law of it."

I nodded. "Thanks," I said, not feeling particularly positive.

. . .

Loch finished the remainder of his drink and patted my back. "I gotta go. We'll catch up later?"

"Yeah," I said. After he left, I took my drink and walked to the huge window overlooking the city. The Crystal Hound was an exclusive lounge in one Wolfheart's tallest skyscrapers, and it certainly had one of the best views of the sprawl. The city lights glittered like a carpet of stars below. I went over the events of the day in my mind, still in a haze of disbelief. It felt like a dream. In fact, I'd had dreams just like this—with him showing back up in my life. I closed my eyes, and I could feel the soft press of his lips on mine. Maybe I shouldn't have kissed him, but it just felt like the natural thing to do. Our lips were calling to one another. Our bodies were, too.

I wanted him so badly. How could I help him? How could I rescue him?

"You look like you're having a rough day," a voice said. I opened my eyes. A dark-haired woman with opal eyes smiled at me from a leather easy chair, her crossed thighs hugged by a tight fitting black dress. She fingered a glimmering diamond necklace as she sipped on a martini. I turned to her.

"Why do you say that?"

"I can see it in your face." She stood and walked over to me, her body all fluid lines. She gazed out the window, and I caught a whiff of her perfume. It sent a tingle of habit through my body—she was the kind of woman I would've gone for in an instant. Sexy, sophisticated, forgettable. "Beautiful view," she said. "I'm surprised I've never come here before."

"Mm." I wasn't really listening. Not like me. Normally, I would've focused my game on her immediately, but right now...

"Let me get you another drink," she said, gesturing towards my near empty glass. I held it up and examined the remainder of whiskey.

"No, thank you," I said. "I've probably already had enough to drink."

"Oh. Well, a water then?"

"Sure."

I walked with her back to the counter, where we both took a seat. She ordered another martini and a glass of water, and I thought about Perry. How long did I even have before he vanished from my life again? Before Gregor Houndfang came and stole him away? I gritted my teeth as anger flushed inside of me.

. . .

"Sometimes it helps if you talk about it," the woman said. "And I'm all ears. My name's Ava."

"Arthur," I said, and shook her hand. "Look, Ava, I don't mean to be rude, but I'm not interested."

She smiled. "All I'm looking for is some good conversation. I can't get it at home, so I come here. That's all I want. No strings attached."

I sighed, and then proceeded to unload the whole story on her. Normally I wouldn't have been so open about my private business with a random stranger, even if I had been trying to sleep with her, but I was boiling over. I needed to vent and, well, she asked for it. Everything just spilled out, and I found myself opening up even more to her than I had with my brother.

"That's about it," I said, swigging down my glass of water. I wanted it to be whiskey, but I really'd had enough.

"Well," she breathed, her eyes wide. I waited for her to back away from me slowly and run out the door. Instead, she flagged the bartender. "One more martini and a glass of water, please."

"Let me get that one," I said, feeling slightly embarrassed, but she refused.

. . .

"I understand his frustration completely," she said. "To be trapped with someone who you despise is a tax on the soul. And I can only imagine how you feel. Being kept from the person you love is probably worse."

"Maybe," I said. "At least I can forget. He has to live with it every day."

"Tell me one thing," she said. "Why are you sitting around in this bar? You should be out there with him."

"Well, he... I..."

She eyed me.

"I don't know," I confessed.

"You should go get your man," she said. "Who cares about anything else? Who even cares what will happen later on? You have a chance to be with him again, right now. If I were you, I'd be fucking his brains out right now." She casually sipped on her martini.

What the hell *was* I doing? *Perry was back*.

. . .

I stood up from my stool, and she grinned.

"Hey, thank you," I said. "You're amazing. Excuse me? Get this woman another drink, anything she wants, put it on my tab."

She laughed. "Good luck," she said in a singsong tone into her martini glass, and I ran out of the lounge, hopped into the elevator, and was soon on my bike riding towards the Windhelm estate.

PERRY

I lay awake, staring at the ceiling of the guest bedroom. I turned to look at Jupiter, who was sleeping quietly beside me. She sucked her thumb and breathed softly. I hoped she was okay—she hadn't spoken much since we'd arrived in Wolfheart.

That kiss...

I sighed and carefully slipped out from under the covers, doing my best not to disturb her. I tucked the blanket up to her chin, and she murmured and turned to the face the other way, still sucking on her thumb. I went over to the window and looked through the blinds, out across the property to the fence that ran around my family's mansion. We lived on a hill just on the outskirts of the city, and could see the twinkling lights of Wolfheart off in the distance.

. . .

I hoped I'd done the right thing, coming here. My confidence that somehow, I'd find a way for Jupiter and me to escape from our situation was waning with each passing moment, but at the very least... At the very least I'd met him again. I shivered and wrapped my arms around myself, remembering the feeling of his arms around my body. The touch of his lips against mine. Was he thinking about me now, too?

Thirteen years ago, Arthur and I had fallen in love. We'd only had a month together as lovers, having spent nearly all of our friendship unable to confess our feelings. I'd gotten so angry with myself, questioning why I couldn't have been a little braver, telling myself that if I hadn't hesitated, we might've had more time to be with one another. Finding him today had really been the last thing I'd been expecting. Seeing him again had never been a part of my plan coming back here. I'd hoped to find sympathy from my father, but... Now it seemed like that wasn't going to happen. I was stuck again. Stuck with no options. Stuck with a love that'd been rekindled from the ashes.

I wanted to see him again. I'd told him not to worry about me, that I thought we should let things be, but that was a lie. I wanted him again. I wanted to see him so badly.

A tear streaked down my cheek, and I quickly wiped it away. *Hounds of Hell... coming back here was a mistake.*

Headlights arced through the fence as a car rolled up the road in front of the house, casting sweeping shadows across the grass. I narrowed my eyes when the car stopped in front of the gate and didn't move. My heart started to pound. The back door to the car opened, and a tall figure stepped out. In the light of the streetlamp I couldn't see his face, but I instantly recognized his silhouette.

"Arthur," I whispered, and I ran out of the room, down the stairs and out the front door. The dewy grass wet my bare feet as I cut down the hill towards the gate. He was pacing back and forth by the car, talking to the driver.

"I don't know, Stephen. Maybe I should climb—" He turned and saw me, and his jaw dropped. "Perry?"

I pulled open the gate and ran to him. I found myself throwing my arms around him, leaping into his arms. I kissed him, unable to restrain myself. He tumbled backwards, banging up against the side of the car. The driver cleared his throat, but we were already too far away, carried off and lost to our desire for one another. For just a moment it felt like it was only him and I in the world, and I felt like it was thirteen years ago and nothing could touch us. I was left breathless, my chest heaving as our lips separated. We gazed into each other's eyes, amazed.

"How did you know I was here?" he asked.

"I didn't. Well, I saw you from the window. But if I hadn't gotten out of bed to look..."

. . .

"Something just keeps bringing us together," he said, grinning. "Something is looking out for us."

"What are you doing here?"

"I've come to get you. If you're gonna have to go back to Elclaw at some point, then at least spend the time you're here with me. Get out of this house. Be with someone who loves you."

"Arthur... I don't..."

"Come with me," he said. His face was strong, confident, kind. I remembered that it was these things that'd attracted me to him in the beginning, that I'd fallen in love with. "Go get Jupiter. You'll be safe at the Luna house. And who knows, maybe we can find a solution to this mess."

"I don't know..." I whispered, almost to myself. It was crazy, but all of this was. Running to Wolfheart, seeing Arthur again... I'd lived obediently for so long that it felt wrong—but I'd already come this far. What the hell was stopping me from going further? "Alright," I said, finally. "Okay. I'll be right back."

. . .

"I'm not going anywhere," Arthur said, and I turned and ran back to the house. I raced up the stairs and back to the bedroom. My suitcase lay on the floor next to Jupiter's, still packed.

"Sweetie," I said, gently shaking her shoulder. She stirred and groaned, her eyes slowly opening.

"Daddy," she murmured.

"I'm going to carry you, okay? You can go back to sleep. Daddy's going to pick you up."

She nodded, stuck her thumb back in her mouth, and closed her eyes. I scooped her up from the bed with one arm and hauled our suitcases with the other. I made my way down the stairs, doing my best not to make any noise.

"Perry," a voice hissed. I froze and turned, and then relaxed when I saw Dimitrius standing in the doorway to his bedroom.

"Why are you awake?" I said. "Go back to sleep."

"It's not even late," he said. "I wasn't even asleep. What's going on? Where are you going?"

. . .

"Keep your voice down," I said. "I can't stay here. Not with Dad."

"Shit, take *me* with you," he said. "*I* can hardly stand the man. Where are you going?"

"The Luna house," I said.

"Luna? Like Master Loch Luna?"

"His brother. Maybe you were too young..."

"Arthur," he said, like the memory had just returned to him. "I remember him. He was your boyfriend in pre-academy. Wow, I'd forgotten."

"I gotta go," I said. "I'll be in contact."

"What do I tell Dad?" he asked.

"You don't need to lie to him," I said. "Don't get into trouble on account of me. Just tell him the truth."

"Fuck that," he grinned. "I'll let him figure it out."

. . .

I smiled and said, "I'll see you around," before hurrying out.

Arthur's driver quickly came around and opened the back door, helping me load Jupiter into the back while Arthur put our luggage into the trunk. Jupiter curled up on the seat, and Arthur produced a blanket and covered her up with it. The driver pulled the car away from the fence, and I took a look back out the window as the house disappeared from view. I knew that this wasn't going to be forever. Fate had brought us back together, but it also would separate us again. It was only a matter of time. It was strange how familiar this felt to thirteen years ago. We'd spent so many days together telling each other that there was no way we'd be separated, that we'd fight, that things would work out because we were in love. I guess the difference was that we knew better, now. I could appreciate this extra time I'd been given with him, however short it might end up being.

I leaned my head on Arthur's arm, his arm wrapped tightly around my shoulder. Jupiter slept curled up on the seat, her head on my lap.

"She's adorable," he said.

"I can't wait for her to meet you."

He leaned in and kissed me. I melted into him, savoring it. Every kiss from him was better than the last. I hardly remembered a kiss being so sweet, so wonderful.

. . .

We arrived at the Luna house, and I followed Arthur through the sprawling mansion with Jupiter in my arms. It was my first time seeing his home, and the difference in family status and wealth was obvious. The Windhelm estate seemed like a tiny little shack in comparison. We walked down huge, ornately trimmed hallways adorned with towering oil paintings of regal looking wolves who stared down at us with stern eyes, past heavy wood doors that guarded room after room. The place was so big, I wouldn't have been surprised if we could hide away here forever without anyone finding us. The silly idea did cross my mind—could I just stay hidden away here forever as his secret?

"Jupiter can sleep in this room," he said, opening a door. "This used to be my younger brother's room. Everyone's moved out except me."

I tucked Jupiter under the covers of the king-sized bed. It was adorable how small she looked sleeping in the middle of such a huge thing. She stirred, but didn't wake, and I kissed her on her forehead.

"Goodnight, sweetie," I whispered, and followed Arthur to his bedroom.

He shut the door and drifted over to me, undoing the buttons of his shirt, one by one. My heart raced as I pulled my shirt up and tugged it off of my head. He opened his at the front, revealing a physique that hadn't been neglected these past thirteen years. I gripped the shirt on either side and helped pull it down his arms, revealing biceps as hard as carved oak. He laid his palms on my chest, sending ripples of goosebumps across my skin, and slowly drew his hands up until they were at my neck. He slipped one hand around the back of my neck and drew me in to him, until my bare chest pressed up against his. The warmth of his skin on mine was intoxicating. I leaned close to him, resting my forehead against his. We held back from the kiss, our lips hovering millimeters apart, the sides of our noses gently touching. I took in his breath and he did mine, like we were living on one another's each and every breath.

Then, finally, we kissed. This one wasn't like the brief reunion kiss we'd shared on the roof, nor was it like the restrained kiss at the car, or the gentle one we'd shared inside it—this was broken floodgates. His hands were on me and mine on him as our lips crashed desperately together. He pushed me back, his greedy hands working at the tie to my pajama bottoms. They were down to my ankles in seconds, and I nearly tripped over myself as I stumbled to get out of them. He caught me, one strong arm around my waist, the other wasting no time to get reacquainted with the hard excitement between my legs. I moaned as his lips found my neck and his hand gripped my bulge. A hard squeeze, like a test, before tugging my underwear down too. I was fully naked, he was still in his trousers, and he gave me a quick shove that sent me bouncing back onto the bed. He gripped his belt, flipping open the buckle and yanking open the front, dropping his trousers down to his ankles. He stepped out of them and pushed his underwear down to follow them. When he straightened upright again I sucked in a breath as I took in the sight of his gorgeous form. Yeah, he *really* hadn't neglected his body these past thirteen years.

I was hungry for him, dying to be reunited with him in the best way. He came forward and I tried to sit up, but he gently pushed me back down by my shoulders. He kissed down from my collarbone, across my chest and to my abs, his lips brushing the trail of hair leading down to my hardened cock. I sighed as his fingers wrapped around me, squeezing me tightly in his fist. Then he lowered his face down, his gaze never leaving mine as he opened his mouth and took me inside of him. I moaned and squirmed against the sheets as he enveloped me in his warmth, his tongue teasing pleasure out of me that had long been neglected.

"Oh, fuck," I murmured. "Arthur...." It was obvious that he still knew exactly how to please me, even after all this time. Or maybe it was just the fact that it was him, and anything he could've done at that moment would've been the best thing I'd ever felt.

He kissed the tip of my cock, swirling his tongue along the curve of my head before giving attention to my balls, gently sucking on them and caressing them with long, velvety licks. I flinched and gasped, my toes curling with every movement. I felt warmth building in my stomach, an aching to be filled as my entrance became wet with an omega's desire.

"I've missed you," he said softly, kissing the pillar of my cock. "I've missed everything about you. I've missed hearing you moan. Tasting you. Feeling you. Perry, I've missed you so fucking much."

"I've missed you too," I whispered. "I had no idea how much I'd missed you until I saw your face again."

He came back up and kissed me, and I held him tightly to me, not wanting to let go. I held on when he sat up, my arms slung around his neck. His cock pressed against my stomach and my own cock, crossing like swords.

"I want to fuck you," he told me, our foreheads pressed together. I kissed him and dropped down to the bed, turning myself around to present my ass to him.

"Then do it," I said.

He reached into his bedside drawer and drew out a condom, unwrapped it, and unfolded it down his length. Then he came onto the bed, moving on his knees until he was right behind me. He caressed my ass cheek with his hand, gently running his palm and fingertips down my skin. I shivered and begged him with my eyes not to keep me waiting. He answered with his cock, taking it firmly in his hand and pressing it up to my opening. Then he entered me. I cried out in surprise as his cock filled me, stretching me out. It'd been such a long time since I'd fucked, and that feeling was like a glass of ice water to sun parched lips. And it was *him*. Arthur Luna. A dream come true.

. . .

Moonlight crossed through the shadows to pool across the bed, casting our lovemaking in a lunar spotlight. Arthur gripped my waist as he thrust into me, his cock pumping deep like the pistons of a wolf-cycle engine. I pushed my face into the sheets, gritting the fabric between my teeth in an effort to hold back the groans of pleasure that were threatening to depart my lips. I was being carried away into a world of ecstasy I'd forgotten—ecstasy and the comfort of being taken by the man I loved.

How had I managed to go without him? How had I done it? It was too good—*he* was too good.

He leaned down and kissed me. I moaned against his lips. "I love you. I love you."

I was going to come. I could feel the tidal wave of climax rushing towards me, about to eclipse me and drown me in an ocean of pleasure. Arthur fucked me harder, gritting his teeth as his muscles tensed and rippled with every thrust. Beads of sweat glistened against his chest, and I could see he was going to come too. I let myself go. I moaned into the sheets as the orgasm hit me, and my cock throbbed and came. Arthur's gasp sounded almost like one of shock. He gripped my ass cheek with one strong hand and thrust in deep, all the way to the hilt, and I could feel his cock swelling and pulsing inside of me with his finish.

. . .

I crumpled into the bedsheets, and Arthur fell next to me, both of us gasping for breath. I looked at him, and he smiled at me between breaths, sweat matting his hair. I reached over and pushed a lock of dark hair from his forehead and kissed him.

"I love you too," he said, his smile turning into a grin.

After cleaning up the mess we'd made on the bed, Arthur and I took a shower together and then cuddled up under the covers. I nuzzled into his chest and nibbled on his collarbone, just like I used to do. I was amazed at how easy it was to fall back into old habits, even after all of this time. It was like picking up right where we left off.

"Do you remember the first time we had sex?" I asked him.

"I do," he said. "It wasn't nearly as comfortable as this. It was on top of that announcer's building. Our knees got all banged up."

I laughed. "It was the only place we could meet. Every time we did it, we hurt ourselves even more. It looked like we'd fallen off a motorcycle, or something."

"That was the most intense month of my entire life," he said. I caught a hint of wistfulness in his voice.

. . .

"Yeah," I said, recalling the memories. "I remember being so angry at first, when you first admitted you were in love with me. I remember thinking, 'why couldn't he have said something earlier?' We'd been friends for years. Why wait until a month before I was going to be married?"

"I was afraid," he said. "I was worried I'd ruin the friendship. It took me that long to realize how dumb of an excuse that was."

I laughed. "But I understand, completely. I was afraid, too. That's why I never said anything. I was afraid that if we got together, I'd have to live with losing you for the rest of my life."

"I guess we had to deal with that anyway," he said, sadly.

"I don't regret that time together at all," I told him. "Not one bit. No matter how hard it was afterwards."

"Mm."

I looked at him. "Do you?"

"No," he said. "But it was hard. And now that you're here, and I'm next to you, I'm remembering just how hard it was. It changed me."

. . .

"How?"

"I realized today that I'd lost the ability to fall in love with anyone. Anyone but you."

I felt a bittersweet pang grip my heart. I hugged him close. "Surely you must've found others."

"I tried. I've met lots of women, some of them more special than others. But many of them I had just because I could. And I could never bring myself to be with another omega after you."

"I see," I said, uncertain how to feel. It hurt to hear how he'd been suffering. I'd hoped that at least he would've found happiness even if I couldn't.

"I know," he said. "I'm broken in that way."

"It's an empty feeling, living a life without love," I said. "I dealt with that for ten years, until I had my daughter. She saved me."

"And now, you're trying to save her."

. . .

"Before it's too late," I said. "Yes. But I think I may have gotten my hopes up." I shivered, feeling a dark cloud of hopelessness pulling over me. "I don't think anything can be done."

Arthur hugged me close to him. I could hear the beating of his heart through his chest, my face rising and falling with every breath.

"I won't let him take you and Jupiter back," he announced.

I smiled. "I appreciate you wanting to comfort me. But you and I both know that it's not that simple. I'm an omega, he's an alpha. I belong to him."

Arthur sighed. "We'll see."

I kissed his chest, then his neck, then his cheek, and finally his lips. "No matter what happens, I'm glad to be here with you. Everything will have been worth it just because I got to see you."

"It's not over," he said quietly. "It's just beginning."

We lay together in each other's arms for a while, just enjoying each other's presence and touch. The moonlight slowly tiptoed its way up the bed and across the wall as the hours trickled by. I didn't know what would happen tomorrow. I was afraid that all of this would be over, as quick as it had come back together. Whenever I glanced at Arthur's face, thinking he must've dozed off by now, I saw his eyes were open. I realized he probably was thinking the same thing I was.

"Arthur," I whispered.

"Yeah?"

"I should go to the other room. Jupiter won't know where she is in the morning."

"Okay."

Leaving his arms felt like the most painful thing, like my body was crying out to return to his embrace. I slowly slid out from the covers and he followed me, taking my hand. I realized what this felt like—the last day we'd spent together back then. Every moment of that day we'd wanted to be in each other's arms, unwilling to let go of each other's hands, hoping that maybe if he held on tight enough everything would turn out okay.

"I'll be here tomorrow," I reassured him, knowing he was having the same fears and feelings as me. He relaxed.

. . .

"Goodnight," he said. "I'll see you tomorrow." And he smiled, like he was delighted to hear himself speak those words.

"Tomorrow," I repeated, and disappeared into the other room.

Jupiter was curled up under the covers, sleeping peacefully. A kiss of moonlight splashed across her forehead, and I went and drew the curtains shut and slid under the covers next to her. Despite the wild turn the day had brought, and all the fresh uncertainty that came with it, I felt calmer at that moment than I had in a very long time.

* * *

The next morning, I woke up and gave Jupiter a bath before laying out some of my clothes on the bed to change. Jupiter bounced up and down on the huge bed, giggling as she rolled around. She was unable to complete a full shift yet, but she had figured out how to pop out her ears and tail, so she wiggled around with just a set of wolf pup ears and a fluffy grey tail.

"Do we live here, Daddy?"

"No, sweetie," I said, buttoning up my shirt. "We're just staying here for now. This is Daddy's good friend's place."

. . .

"Oh. I like the bed." She laughed and plopped down into the billowy comforter, her little tail wagging.

Suddenly, the door to the bedroom opened. I turned around, grinning, expecting to see Arthur, but was surprised to see someone else. He was around Arthur's age, probably a little younger, and holding on to his hand was a little girl around five years old. I immediately could see the family connection—this was one of Arthur's brothers.

"Uhh, hello," he said, freezing. "Who are you?"

"Hello," I said, "I'm Perry Houndfang." Part of me wanted to use my bachelor name, Windhelm, but it probably wouldn't have been proper. "Um, Arthur put me and my daughter up in this room."

"I'm Vander," he said, shaking my hand. "This is my daughter, Alexis."

Jupiter sat in the middle of the bed, watching quietly. She always became very quiet around other people. Alexis walked over and climbed up onto the bed, and Jupiter eyed her cautiously.

"Isn't my daddy's bed fun?" Alexis asked. "It's so big, and poofy. Look what I can do on it." She started to bounce up and down, and at the peak of her jump she shifted, to my surprise, into a bear cub. Vander's mate was a bear, apparently. She bounced back onto the bed, and Jupiter's eyes widened. She started to laugh, her tail wagging furiously.

"Do it again!" she squealed.

I smiled. "Vander," I repeated. "Oh, this is your room! I'm so sorry."

"No worries," Vander said. "Arthur didn't know we'd be home. You're... I know you." His eyes widened. "You're *that* omega!"

I laughed. "That omega?"

"Sorry, I didn't mean to be rude. It's just that, we kinda just had a conversation about why Arthur wouldn't date omegas, and—"

He was cut off when Arthur came up next to him and rested his elbow on his shoulder.

"Good morning," Arthur said loudly.

I took one look at his hair and started to laugh.

"What?" he asked.

"Your bed hair," I said, pointing.

Vander turned to look, and snorted. "You look like your hair exploded."

Alexis squealed with laughter too as she jumped up and down on the bed. Jupiter went quiet again with the new addition to the room, and came to hide behind my leg.

"You look silly, uncle Arthur," Alexis said.

Arthur quickly ran his hands through his hair, but it only made it worse. I laughed harder, and he groaned. "Ah, screw it. Vander, what the hell are you doing home?"

"I remembered how much I missed it, yesterday. Hey, I thought you'd be happy to see your little brother. Loch's going to be here later, too, if you weren't aware."

"I knew that," Arthur said. "Sorry, I'll move Perry and Jupiter to Christophe's room."

"Nah," Vander replied. "That's fine. We're not staying the night. Alexis, let's go and eat some breakfast. You can play with your new friend later. Nice to meet you, Perry," he said, and winked at me.

"Bye," Alexis said, waving to Jupiter. Jupiter silently waved back, her eyes still wide as she gripped my leg.

"Sorry about that," Arthur said. "I had no idea they'd be here today."

"Don't apologize," I said. "I'm the one intruding..."

"You're not," he said. "So. You must be Jupiter." He crouched down to her height, and she hid herself further behind my leg, her ears flattening down and her tail drooping shyly.

"Jupiter, come on. This is Daddy's friend."

"I like your ears," Arthur said. "And your tail. Very nice. I can do that too." He closed his eyes, and his ears pulled upwards to the top of his head, popping out as two, fur-covered wolf ears. He smiled and made them twitch, and Jupiter eased out a bit, her tail wagging curiously.

"Can you shift anything else?" he asked, and she shook her head.

. . .

"That's okay. You'll be able to soon. Are you hungry?"

She nodded.

"Good. Breakfast is ready downstairs, and afterwards you and Alexis can play together. How about that?"

"Okay," she said quietly.

After Arthur washed up and fixed his hair, the three of us went downstairs to join his family in the dining room. In the light of day, the house seemed even more regal and impressive. Gigantic windows lit sprawling sitting rooms lined with towering bookshelves, antique furniture, and artwork. Contrasting the older, antique rooms were modern ones with clean design and cutting-edge style, obviously packed with impressive technology. It was apparent the house was very old, and had been updated and renovated over many decades. You could see family history lying in every corner.

I'd been briefly introduced to his parents before when we were young, but my memory of them was thin. I was worried that they would be apprehensive about having me here, especially because they didn't know who I was, but I was quickly relieved of my fears. They both greeted Jupiter and me warmly, almost as if we were part of the family.

. . .

Arthur exchanged a look with me. I could read the question in his gaze—if it was appropriate for him to discuss my situation. I nodded to him.

"I offered to take Perry and his daughter in because of the situation he's currently in," Arthur said.

"And what situation is that?" Mr. Luna asked.

"My husband," I said. "Is not a faithful man. Nor is he a reliable father, or a kind one. My mother and father had arranged my marriage to him when I was very young, in order to strengthen our family position. I managed to hold on out of duty to my family, but once I had Jupiter... I couldn't stand having her raised in that environment, so I took her and left. I was hoping to find a way to sever the marriage, but my father isn't supportive, and I've come to realize that there isn't a way to do it anyway."

"Perry and I are in love," Arthur announced, suddenly. I looked at him in shock.

"Well, I think we all knew that," Mrs. Luna said.

"I didn't know that," Mr. Luna said, looking bemused.

. . .

"*Perry* was the only omega he was ever with. You must've had a great effect on Arthur for him to never want to be with another omega."

I felt myself blushing. "Um, well..."

Arthur groaned. "Mom..."

Vander started laughing, and Alexis looked around the table, curious to know what joke she didn't get. Jupiter quietly munched on some cereal, in her own world.

"You *are* right," Mr. Luna said, his expression serious. "A marriage bond is sacred. As unfortunate as the situation may be, the promise made between your families isn't something that can be broken."

"There must be some way, Dad," Arthur said.

He shook his head. "Unless it's a mutual agreement, I don't know of any way. The alpha must approve of the decision."

"That's ridiculous," Vander said. "That's backwards."

"Being highborn often is," Mr. Luna said.

. . .

I had expected this to be the case, so I hadn't gotten my hopes up, but I could see Arthur had. He looked at me, a furious determination burning in his eyes. All I could do was take his hand in mine, and try to transfer some of the peace I felt to him through my touch. *At least I found you again.*

ARTHUR

After breakfast, Vander took Alexis and Jupiter to go play, and Perry and I went to the sitting room to speak. Mom and Dad seemed unusually calm about the situation, considering how sudden it all was. I realized that they both understood the significance this had to me. With my track record when it came to prospective mates, they'd been worried that I would continue to shirk commitments and only go after casual romances. Honestly, if it wasn't Perry, it couldn't be anyone else. I only now consciously understood that was the reason why I couldn't seem to care about any of the people I slept with. As pathetic as it was, I'd been hung up on him this whole time, only now I saw it for it what it was. If Perry was taken away from me this time, maybe I wouldn't even bother trying again.

"I wish there was something more we could do," Mom said. "But for now, we can at least do what we can to provide sanctuary here."

. . .

"Joseph would never challenge me," Dad said, speaking of Perry's father. "He's not going to try and force you to come home, unless he's willing to risk ridicule in the community."

"He won't," Perry said. "Mom might've, but my dad has no backbone."

Dad stroked his chin. "What we can try is to make an offer to your husband. He'll come here, or send someone eventually to fetch you. Perhaps he'll be willing to agree to some terms to void your marriage."

After finishing speaking with my parents, Perry and I went back to my bedroom. He sat down on the edge of the bed and I joined him, putting my arm around him.

"I feel good about this," I said. "My parents want to help you."

He nodded, but he didn't look very hopeful.

"What is it?" I asked.

"Gregor may not be in love with me, but he *is* in love with the power he holds over me and our daughter. That's what he loves more than anything else. The control. *Especially* the control he has over Jupiter. At least I can see what he's doing. I can resist his manipulation and his mind games, but Jupiter can't. It's warping her, and eventually it'll break her. I wish I could believe that offering him something as an exchange would work, but I just don't think that anything will make him want to give that up."

The rage stewed inside me like boiling water in a pressurized pot. I hated this helpless feeling, but I had to keep it together for Perry. Whatever I felt was nothing compared to what he was going through. This was what he'd been dealing with for thirteen years.

"Arthur... I hate that I've suddenly dragged you and your family into this mess. It isn't fair that I just showed back up in your life and brought all this misery with me."

"It isn't fair that you have to deal with this shit," I said. "Perry, I've been lost this whole time without you, and I didn't even realize it. I will *fight* to the end. No matter what the outcome."

There was a knock on the bedroom door. It was Vander, and his eyes were wide with eager excitement.

"What is it?" I asked.

"Loch and Tresten are here. And he thinks he might've found a way to help you guys."

. . .

Perry and I exchanged a puzzled look and hurried alongside Vander to the sitting room. Mom, Dad, Loch, and Tresten were seated inside, talking quietly while Alexis and Jupiter both sat on the floor with Ian, who was reading a book to them.

Loch stood. "Stephen," he said, "Could you please have the kids entertained for a little while?"

"Certainly, sir," Stephen said, emerging from a corner of the room with two other house staff.

"Daddy will be here," Perry said, smiling at Jupiter, who looked to him for approval. "Go have some fun."

I gave Loch a quick hug. "You've actually found something? So soon? It's not having a bunch of fighters beat the shit out of him, is it? Because I wouldn't object to that."

"Me neither," Perry muttered.

"Close," Loch said, smirking. "I spoke to Master Graffer and some of the other fighter masters at the school this morning, and I was told about 'the rite of challenge.' Apparently, it's actually an old highborn law."

. . .

Dad laughed. "The rite of challenge? Like when you fought the Bellock boy, Loch? I thought that was just a Fighting Arts School custom."

"Yes, but there's also an official *law* regarding it," Loch said. "An ancient one, still in effect, even though it's not really in use anymore."

"Fighting to the death isn't as glorious as it once was," Tresten said.

"So... *I* have to beat the shit out of him?"

"I mean you could... But the law applies to almost any other measurable challenge where the two people are on equal competitive ground. You submit an official notice of challenge with the terms, and it's distributed amongst the leading members of both party's clans."

"What happens if I lose the challenge?" I asked. "If it's not a fight to the death?"

"Uh, well... I guess, nothing," Loch said. "Apart from any loss of respect and honor in the eyes of the clans."

"Hrm." I looked to Perry. "What do you think about this?" I was skeptical—outside of trained fighters, nobody talked about dueling or challenges unless it had to do with an old story. It was hard for me to imagine something like that being officially recognized by the law these days.

"I don't think Gregor would ever accept a challenge to a fight," Perry said. "He'd know he'd lose."

"It does have to be on equal ground," Loch said.

"If it were an equal challenge, though... And the eyes of the clan were on him... He cares a lot about his status in Elclaw. If he turned down a fair challenge, he'd lose honor amongst the clan, and that *might* be enough for him to compel him to accept."

"So, what's an equal challenge?" Mom asked, and added in a quiet voice, "Something not too dangerous."

At that moment, it came to me. "A wolf-cycle race. That's it. He's a racer, too. A well-known one in Elclaw. That would be double the shame if he turned down a racing challenge."

Perry's eyes widened. "Hounds of Hell..."

"I think this might be it!" I said.

. . .

"A wolf-cycle race," Mom said, sounding faint.

"What do we need to do to start the process?" I asked Loch, a grin plastered on my face. My body thrummed with so much excitement, I was trembling. *There was hope.*

As the leader of our clan, my brother Christophe was called to come oversee the drafting of the challenge and to put his official endorsement on it. While we were waiting, Perry pulled me aside.

"I don't know how I feel about you doing this," he said. "You'd be risking your safety out on that track for me..."

"I risk my safety every time I race," I told him. "This time will be no different."

"If you get hurt? Or worse? I don't know what I'd do."

"I won't." I took his hands in mine. "Don't worry."

"I hate feeling so useless. This is my battle to fight, and you're doing it for me."

"We're doing it together. You've been fighting for a long time, Perry. Look, I don't believe it was just chance that you found me yesterday. It's obvious we've both been trying to get back to each other this whole time. This is how it's meant to be. *We're* meant to be. We've been given a real chance. So let's make this work."

He nodded and hugged me tightly. "I love you, Arthur," he said. "I've never stopped loving you all this time." He touched my cheek and drew me into a kiss.

We kissed again, long and sweet. My heart overflowed with love for him, a feeling so incredible and overwhelming in both its foreignness to me and its power. *This is how love feels. Remember?*

By the end of the day, a copy of it was already submitted to the other ranking members of our clan, and the main, paper copy was en route to Elclaw, along with a digital copy sent directly to Gregor Houndfang and the leaders of the Silver Sun Clan. There'd be no avoiding it—the challenge was out in the world, and would soon be seen and acknowledged by both our clans.

I could win this. I could help Perry and Jupiter.

* * *

The tires of my wolf-cycle tore up a cyclone of dirt and debris as I gunned the engine, ripping up the weeds and overgrowth that littered the Golden Forest Proving Ground. The White Tree track was only open on certain days for practice and training runs, and I wanted to get as much wheel time as I could. The truth was that while I was skilled, I was not a professional racer, and Gregor was. In fact, I'd never even seen him race before. That didn't worry me. I'd beaten top professionals in open races before.

Stephen hired a team to help us set up monitoring electronics so that Perry could act as my pit crew and track guide, watching my runs from a trackside monitor piping in a live feed shot by a drone hovering far above the track. Perry may not have been a racer himself, but he still had extensive knowledge of the sport and of racing technique. It felt amazing to be working as a team with him, like a dream come true. That was really what the past few days had been —a dream come true.

"Watch the upcoming corner," Perry's voice buzzed in the speaker clipped to my ear.

"Copy that," I growled, my voice the graveling tone of a wolf's. I tilted my left front paw while lifting up just ever so slightly with my rear right one, sending my bike arcing around the corner. On the heads-up display projected on the panoramic cockpit window was a map of the track, along with several data readouts. A targeting reticle blinked a warning to me, showing a pothole in the track. With my enhanced senses, I'd detected it far earlier and swerved easily to avoid it.

"Damn track is coming apart," I said.

. . .

"Careful out there. Wouldn't want to lose the challenge before Gregor even responds to us."

"Funny," I said, gunning the throttle and pulling into The Walls obstacle. Gravity pulled at me as my bike curved up the slanted track, exploding through vines that hung down the sides. With the size of the wolf-cycle and the speed I was driving, running through the debris felt as soft as the vibration of rain on a windshield. The difficulty with practicing here instead of at White Tree was that we were missing certain obstacles, and others were far less treacherous. For example, The Forest obstacle here only had three rows of pylons, a quick pass-through compared to the hundreds that were at White Tree.

"What kind of racer is Gregor?" I asked.

"Don't talk, concentrate on your driving," Perry said.

"I should probably know these things," I said, following the hairpin zig-zags of the track and narrowly dodging a family of squirrels trying to crack acorns on the asphalt.

"He's... fearless when going into the obstacles. Sharp, with amazing reaction time. Has great ability to read the track and his opponents. Don't underestimate him."

. . .

"I don't intend to."

"That said, he's good, but he's not perfect. You definitely have a fair shot... As long as you keep practicing."

I laughed. "Not the most encouraging words."

"His weakness is his pride—and that desire to control. Goad him into making a mistake."

I banked into the last straightway, roaring toward The Forest. A plume of dust rose up in my wake, like the tail of a huge wolf. I entered The Forest, quickly swerving around the pylons, cutting as close to them as I could. I liked to imagine that if I were in human form, I could stick a hand out and graze each one with my fingertips. Of course, if I actually did that I'd lose my arm. They whipped by with a loud *FWOOMP* sound, and I exited the obstacle and crossed over the weathered checkered finish line. I pulled my bike into the pit, where Perry was waiting for me by the monitors.

"Good run," he said as I stepped out of the bike and padded towards him. He stroked my muzzle, which became my cheeks as I shifted back to human form. "Cleaner than the last three. But still a long way to go. We've got a lot of training to do."

. . .

"Fine by me," I said. "But it might help if I had a reward. Something to look forward to after each race."

He gave me an amused look. "Oh, really?"

"Yeah. Got anything you can give me?"

Perry gripped my chin with his thumb and forefinger and pulled me into a kiss. "There's a couple things..."

I felt his other hand slip down between my legs and grab a hold of my package.

"You seem excited," he said, and I grinned.

"Nothing like racing at three hundred miles an hour to get the blood flowing."

He smirked and kissed me again, pushing me back toward the bike until my back slammed against the side of it. Perry grabbed the zipper of my skintight racing suit, and in one quick motion pulled it down from where it started at my neck, all the way down to the bottom of my abs. He pushed it open, revealing my naked torso beneath it, and slipped his hand down my front until it tucked into the suit and met my throbbing hard cock. I wasn't joking—it wasn't unusual for me to get horny as hell when racing. Something about all that danger and speed and the adrenaline pumping through my body made me want to fuck, and watching the action did the same for Perry. In fact, I remembered the way he used to fuck me after we'd spent the day watching races at the track, and it made me even more turned on.

I pushed the racing suit down my waist so that I was fully exposed, and Perry dropped to his knees in front of me. He looked up into my eyes as he grasped the base of my cock and quickly flicked his tongue across the head, drawing out a glimmering strand of precome. Then, without wasting another moment, he opened his mouth and drank me down his throat. I slapped my hand against the side of the bike to steady myself as my knees shook, unsteadied by the incredible pleasure that surged through my body from his mouth.

"Oh, shit," I murmured. "Perry..."

He ran his lips up and down my glistening length, caressing it in all the right spots with his tongue. He went at me with such an obvious hunger, like he'd been starving for me, or like he was trying to make up for all the lost time. My legs were trembling from his attention, and I jerked and nearly slid down the side of the wolf-cycle's engine compartment. With one hand I hit the door release, opening up the inner cockpit of the bike. It was cramped for a fully shifted wolf, but for two puny humans it was just the right size to have some fun. Perry took me out of his mouth, and I helped him to his feet and kissed him, my tongue dancing against his, tasting my flavors leftover there. I grabbed him and lifted him up and he threw his legs around my waist, and I lowered him into the cockpit of the bike as I quickly undressed him. When he was naked, Perry grabbed me by my shoulders and flipped me onto my back so that he was on top.

"You've done enough riding for today," he said. "My turn."

Straddling me, he reached down and pumped my cock with his fist. I tossed my head back and moaned, and then felt the warmth of his entrance push against my crown. He watched as he lowered himself down on me, gritting his teeth as my bare cock breached him, sliding inch by inch into him until he was at the hilt. He sat there, his mouth opened in a silent gasp, his forehead wrinkled in a look of astonished pleasure. I gazed up at him, and we enjoyed a moment just like that, connected and motionless, my cock pulsing deep inside of him.

Then he started to move his hips, drawing them up and down, riding me slowly. He gripped his hands in mine, steadying him as he started to bounce a little faster on my cock. In the position he was in, his cock sat in perfect reach of me, swinging up and down with every jump of his body. I grasped it and stroked him in synchronization with his movements, and he squeezed my hand and moaned loudly and started to fuck me even harder.

"Fuck," he moaned, "That so feels so good, Arthur. Keep doing that. Please keep doing that..."

. . .

I obeyed, enjoying the look of ecstasy on his face as he rode me. He was gripping me tightly with his entrance, and every movement of his body sent shockwaves of pleasure through me.

"My turn," I said. "Come here."

I sat up, my cock still buried deep inside of him, and flipped him onto his back so that his head lay beneath the steering column, where my paws would go. I pushed his knees back, and steadying myself with one arm, started to thrust into him while continuing to stroke him with my free hand.

"Arthur..." he gasped between my thrusts. "Can you..."

"Hm?"

"Turn it on? The bike?"

I grinned and stood up, withdrawing out of him. He lay on the floor of the cockpit, panting. In my human form, the instrument panel seemed like it'd been made for a giant, and I guess that was true. Leaving the bike in a neutral gear, I flipped up the ignition cover and slammed my palm onto the switch. The bike shuddered and then roared to life, its engine growling like a thousand angry wolves. The power of the engine thrummed through the cockpit, vibrating everything with its energy. Perry squirmed on the floor, begging me to come back to him with his eyes. I buried myself into him again, pounding him deep and hard. His mouth opened in a moan that was muffled by the sound of the idling engine. I reached up and jammed my fist into the accelerator, revving the engine. The vibrations rocked our bodies, and it felt like they were being focused down to where our bodies met, intensifying the sensation of our lovemaking. Then I saw the words on his lips, impossible to hear over the sound of the revving engine.

I'm going to come!

I was at the finish too, and the engine roared and shook the bike with violent power as I came. I felt Perry tighten around me as his eyes widened with climax, and his cock pulsed and sent an arc of come up and across his own chest. I buried myself deep into him, all the way, my cock throbbing and knotting with my orgasm, filling him up with my raw come. He threw his arms around me and pulled me down to kiss him, our lips colliding desperately together as our tongues met and played.

Slowly, I withdrew from him, both of us gasping for breath. I reached up and hit the kill switch, and the engine came to a grumbling stop. We were left with a void of silence that was filled only by the sound of our breathing.

"I love you," Perry said. "I love you, I love you, I love you."

. . .

A sharp ache gripped my heart, hearing him say those words, but I savored it. It meant this was real, and this was rare. I kissed him, never wanting to be apart.

* * *

Jupiter toddled along as fast as her two little legs would carry her. She had her ears and tail shifted out, and today she'd even managed to reveal her wolf's nose. It was cute seeing her running along with her tail wagging and her nose like a little spot of coal in the middle of a pink face. It'd been three days since we'd sent out the challenge, and things had already fallen into a comfortable rhythm in Luna manor. My brothers and their families had stopped in every day, and I could tell my parents were pleased about that.

Over the past few years, everyone else had sort of drifted into their own lives. Loch and Tresten were teaching, and their son was already getting ready to enter pre-academy. Vander and Pell spent a lot of time up north with the bears, working their healing clinic and raising Alexis. Even Christophe, who was still bound to the Luna manor due to his duties as clan leader, spent a lot more time in his own modest home with Mason and Kota. I didn't blame him for wanting to get away. It could be stifling here, and even though he was leader, it was easy to feel not in control of things when living with our parents. Our situation had created an occasion to come visit and lend support. Loch and Tresten were especially supportive. Loch had dueled in a challenge for honor before, and they both understood what it was like to be signed away in an arranged marriage.

. . .

We went outside, and Perry and I watched Jupiter run around in the grassy field by the apple orchard that stretched out into the mountains bordering our home. Perry took my hand, and we walked along, enjoying cool breezes that moved the grass like ripples on the surface of a pond. For a moment, I had a vision of what life would've been like if he and I had always been together. Walks like this together every day. Endless moments of happiness at each other's side. How different would my life have been if we had found a way to be together back then? Thinking of all the empty relationships I'd had over the years made me feel slightly sorry for myself, and upset for those who I'd hurt in my wake. I'd been hurting all this time, and just hadn't realized it. I'd only been trying to fill the space he'd left.

I had the sudden realization that I wouldn't have changed anything. The way life had unfolded had still blessed me with experiences I valued, and most importantly, with a deep appreciation for what Perry and I shared. I knew it was special back then, but seeing how I felt about him now, I understood just how important he was. Just what our love meant. Having experienced the void, I could appreciate the meaning in it all. And, I'd also found myself smitten by little Jupiter. Seeing her curiosity and joy as she explored the world had brought me a lot of joy, too. I wanted to protect her. I wanted to show her things that her alpha father had failed to show her, and to heal whatever wounds he might've inadvertently caused. She was still shy with me and most everyone else except for Perry, but she had made fast friends with Alexis, and after just a few days of being together the two girls seemed to have adopted a sibling relationship. Jupiter followed Alexis around, silently watching everything the older girl did, sometimes imitating her. Alexis was boisterous and playful, so it seemed like a positive match. I couldn't help but find myself thinking of how great an environment this family would be for Jupiter to grow up in.

"Have you heard from your dad?" I asked Perry. "Or your brother, at least?"

"I spoke to Dimitrius on the phone the other day. It sounded like Dad was just glad to get this 'mess' out of his hair."

"I don't want to get ahead of ourselves," I said, "but maybe we should start talking about what might happen after the challenge. Once you and Gregor are separated."

Perry squeezed my hand and smiled at me apologetically. "We *still* haven't even gotten a response back," he said.

"Yeah, but we will. He can't ignore it. And I was thinking that your brother could join us here sometime. Be a part of things. Especially for afterwards. He's Jupiter's uncle, after all."

"Wow, you are getting ahead of yourself," Perry laughed. He poked my side. "Just what do you think is going to happen, anyway?"

"We're going to get married," I said.

. . .

"Are we?" He smirked at me.

"Yes. Do you not want to?"

"Is this a proposal?"

I laughed and threw my arm around his shoulder. "Stop teasing me."

"I'm not teasing you," he said, grinning. "I'm serious."

"Okay, fine." I took his hands and dropped to one knee. "Perichor Windhelm, will you marry me?" and quickly added, "If everything works out?"

Perry laughed, pulled me to my feet, and kissed. "You're damn right I will. And of course Dimitrius will be a part of things."

"What about your father?"

"What *about* my father?"

. . .

"He is your father, and Jupiter's grandfather."

"And Gregor is Jupiter's 'father'. It doesn't change his actions, nor does it entitle him to any right to be a part of Jupiter's life. He's failed us too many times. He's failed *me* too many times."

I nodded, not wanting to press the subject any further. I knew why Perry felt this way—his mother and father had been directly responsible for the choices that'd led to his unhappiness—but it was still difficult for me to fully understand. I'd been raised with the belief that family—flesh and blood—be always given a certain level of respect, regardless of misunderstandings or differences. This belief conflicted with my thoughts about Gregor, too. He didn't deserve to be a part of Jupiter's life, but he was her flesh and blood. If she did become my daughter, what would I do later in life when she asked about her birth father? Would I want him to have a place in her life, even after the things he'd done?

"Arthur! Daddy! Look!"

Perry and I exchanged a glance, and ran over to where Jupiter was standing in the tall grass. It was the first time she'd ever called to me by my name.

She held up her hands to show us—except they weren't hands, they'd shifted into paws. She giggled as she waved them in the air, and then they popped back into human form. She looked at them, disappointed.

"Aw. I had paws."

"I saw," I said, crouching down. "Can I see your hands?"

She came over to me, leaned against my leg, and placed her hands in my palms. I glanced up at Perry, and he nodded to me in happy acknowledgement. Jupiter had never been this comfortable with me before.

I turned her hands over, looking at both sides. She still had her ears, nose, and tail shifted out, and she looked at me with wide eyes, her tail wagging curiously.

"Close your eyes," I said. "Think about your hands becoming paws again. Picture it in your head. Can you do that?"

"Okay."

She closed her eyes. Almost immediately, she became completely human again. Then, fur pushed from the back of her hands, and her fingers fused to become paws. She opened her eyes and squealed happily. Then she tapped her paws on top of her head and her butt, and frowned, disappointed.

. . .

"Aww. I lost the other stuff."

"Yes, but you were able to control the shift. That's a very good sign, Jupiter. You know what it means?"

She shook her head.

"It means that you're almost ready to complete a full shift." I stood up, and Jupiter's paws shifted back to hands. She reached up and took my hand, holding on to three of my fingers. She squeezed her eyes shut, straining, and her ears popped up from the top of her head. She touched them, and looked very pleased with herself.

"She's going to be able to complete her first shift, soon," I told Perry.

"I'm going to need to arrange a ceremony," he said. He looked flustered. "I don't have anyone to perform it..."

"Perry," I said, taking his hand. Jupiter looked up at us, glancing back and forth between us with curious eyes. "We're a *team*. Okay? It doesn't matter if you're still married to Gregor. In my mind, we're already together. I know my family would be more than happy to perform the ceremony for Jupiter."

. . .

I didn't say it out loud, but I knew that eventually, my family would be Jupiter's family. I was sure of it. So, it was more than appropriate for us to do the rites of the first shift for her, to witness the most important first step in any shifter's life—especially when she had no one else.

PERRY

The ceremony for Jupiter's first shift was set up in one of the spare ballrooms in the Luna estate, and the room was filled with hundreds of candles and other ritual items to help her complete her very first transformation. It was adorable to watch Arthur interacting with her, telling her what she could expect from her first shift. I was surprised to see how quickly she'd opened to him. Maybe it had to do with the environment, being away from Elclaw and the horrible energy that always permeated our house there, but she seemed to be thriving here even after just a few days. She'd made new friends with Arthur's niece and nephews, and she was speaking more than I'd ever heard her talk before.

I still remained hesitant about getting my hopes up. Arthur had already began planning for the future—our future—but the world had a way of kicking you down just when things were looking up. I'd been kicked too many times. But it was hard. Hounds of Hell, it was hard. Especially watching

Jupiter with him. He was so good with her, so much more the father that she needed. Deep down, I wanted to be hopeful, and I constantly felt that feeling rising up in me like a geyser.

And what really worried me was the lack of any word from Gregor or the Silver Sun Clan. It'd been nearly a week. Why hadn't he responded? There'd been nothing from him. It almost seemed like he hadn't even noticed Jupiter and I had gone. That should've been a good thing, but it made me nervous. The uncertainty of everything, the clock ticking towards some doom I felt was lurking there. That was probably his intention, though. That was how Gregor worked. He knew it had to be eating away at me, wondering when he'd come for us. He knew exactly how to pick at me, what would get to me the most.

"Hey," Arthur said, coming over to me. "You okay?"

"Mm. Yeah, I'm fine," I said.

"Okay." He kissed me. "Loch told me he's on his way from the Academy, your brother is with him. We'll get the ceremony started as soon as they get here. She's ready."

Random parts of Jupiter's body had begun to spontaneously shift, which meant she was close. The candles flickered around the room, and sweet-smelling smoke floated up from their wicks, filling the room in a fragrant haze. At first,

Jupiter looked uneasy about the whole thing, until Alexis arrived and reassured her with her happy-go-lucky attitude.

"I did this," she told Jupiter. "You don't have to be scared. It's easy. And I'll be there with you, too."

"Okay," Jupiter said quietly. She came to me and pulled at my hand. "Daddy..."

"What is it, sweetie?"

"What if I can't shift?"

I crouched down and stroked her hair, pushing it back behind her ear. "Don't worry about that," I told her. "You're gonna do fine. Arthur's been showing you how to do it, right?"

She nodded. "Yes."

"Well, then. And everyone is going to be there with you. Even Uncle Dimitrius."

"Is Father going to be there?"

. . .

My throat tightened. I chewed the inside of my lip. "No, sweetie."

"Okay," she said, and she looked relieved. "Will Arthur?"

"Yes. Of course."

"Okay." She looked a little more confident hearing that, and it made my heart glad.

"Masters Loch and Dimitrius have arrived," Stephen announced to the room. "They will be here in just a few minutes. We'll be starting the ceremony soon."

We changed into ceremonial robes, and Loch and Dimitrius entered not too long after. Dimitrius looked intimidated to be in his teacher's house, and the look on his face was probably the exact same one I'd had on the first day here. He eased up when he saw me and Jupiter, and hurried over to give both of us hugs.

"Hey, there," he said, tapping Jupiter's nose. "How's my niece?"

"I'm going to shift!" Jupiter announced. "Arthur told me how. And Alexis is going to watch too."

. . .

"Whoa!" he said, his eyes widening. "You're excited, aren't you?" She nodded, and Dimitrius looked up at me. "You weren't kidding! Talkative."

The family gathered in the center of the ballroom, making a circle with their joined hands. Arthur took one of Jupiter's hands and I took the other, and the three of us walked her to the center of the circle where she sat cross-legged. We moved to the side, and Christophe stepped forward.

"We guide Jupiter Houndfang across the threshold into a greater world. The wolf's blood runs within you, and tonight it will be released for the first time, in its full form. The Luna house will witness her transformation."

"Close your eyes, sweetie," I whispered to her. "Do what Arthur showed you now."

She squeezed her eyes shut. She balled her hands into fists and strained. I could see she was concentrating with everything she had. A minute passed, and just when it seemed like nothing was going to happen, her ears shifted and pushed out the top of her head. Then her tail followed, and then her nose.

"Very good," Arthur said. "Keep that picture in your mind..."

. . .

Then, grey fur started to erupt out all over her. Her body began to change shape as bones changed positions and her muscles morphed alongside them. Her tiny fists became paws, which dropped to the floor in front of her. Her nose pushed forward into a snout, and soon a fully shifted wolf pup sat in the middle of the circle. Her eyes were still squeezed shut, her head wobbling slightly from side to side in concentration, her ears flopping slightly. Alexis had started to bounce up and down excitedly.

Christophe produced an ornately framed mirror and held it up in front of Jupiter.

"Open your eyes, sweetie," I said.

She did, and let out a startled yelp when she caught her reflection in the mirror. She twisted her body, trying to get a look at herself, and ended up flopping on the floor. She immediately bounced up onto her paws and started to hop up and down excitedly.

"I did it!" she yelped, and looked surprised at the sound of her voice, which had grown throatier and shrill with the transformation.

"You did it!" Alexis cried, jumping up and down.

. . .

Then, one by one, the rest of us shifted into our wolf forms. I stepped forward first and touched my nose to Jupiter's head.

"Welcome, sweetie," I said. "I'm so proud of you."

Arthur went next, and Jupiter stared up at his huge wolf form. He touched his nose to her head. "See? Nothing to it."

Dimitrius followed him. "It's a whole new world, kid," he said.

After him went Alexis, then Vander and Pell, who towered over everyone else in his bear form. Then Loch, Tresten, and Ian gave her their blessings, followed by Basch and Stella, and finally Christophe, Mason, and Kota. It touched me to see them do this for her. No, for *us*. They'd only known us for such a short time, and they were treating us like family. This was the kind of environment that Jupiter deserved. She deserved a big family full of people who cared for her, and for each other.

Jupiter spent the rest of the evening running around with Alexis and Kota, the three of them playing together in their wolf forms. Jupiter was still getting the hang of running with four legs, and she tripped and tumbled over herself often, but each time was helped up by her friends and kept on going with even more determination. She was so happy here. I'd never seen her look so at ease, so free of worry or timidity.

She really was coming out of her den. I couldn't bear to think of making her go back to Elclaw, back to her father.

That night after putting Jupiter to bed, I went to Arthur's room but found it empty. The house was too big to try and guess where he was, so I dialed the house staff on the room's landline and was told that he was in the third-floor study. I peeked inside, and found him sitting in front of the computer, the blue light of the monitor glimmering off his eyes, which were narrowed and focused. I came over to him and he straightened, surprised by my presence. He was watching wolf-cycle races—Gregor's runs. I touched his shoulder, and he rested his hand on top of mine.

"Hi," I said.

He looked up at me and gave me a distracted smile. "Hey."

"Need to be alone?"

"No, no. It's time for a break." He closed the video and let out a long breath.

"I know I already said it, but thank you for today," I told him. "Thank you for what you did for Jupiter. You and your family."

. . .

"Of course," he said. "I'm glad your brother was able to join us, too."

I sat on the edge of the desk and took Arthur's hands in mine, raising them to my lips. "I loved seeing you with Jupiter today. She's really taken to you. I've never seen her so happy."

"Really?" he said, smiling. He looked so pleased, it was adorable.

"Yes," I said. "She really cares about you. I can see she admires you already. I admire you too. You're doing so much more than you need to."

"Enough of that," he said, scooting forward. He slid his arms around my waist and leaned forward, resting his chin onto my chest. "Not another word."

I stroked my fingers through his hair. "You'd make a great father, you know." Again, that surprised, pleased look. I chuckled. "Don't look so shocked. It's obvious, the way you are with Jupiter."

"Honestly, that's about the last thing I'd expect to hear about myself. Arthur Luna, a good father." He laughed. "Then again, none of the Luna brothers were ever the fatherly type. But we rise to the occasion. We fight for the ones we love. And we make sure they're taken care of."

"You're amazing," I told him. "All of you are."

Arthur stood, his hands gliding down from my waist, to the sides of my thighs, until they came to rest on my knees. He pushed them open and stepped between them, and then tilted my chin up with one finger and brought his lips to mine. "*You're* amazing," he said. "I've never met anyone like you."

"I don't know what's so amazing about me," I said.

"You had the strength to walk away," he said. "To do whatever it took to protect your daughter. You've always had that strength. You've always stood out, Perry. That's why I fell in love with you in the first place."

He kissed me again. Hounds of Hell, I loved him so much. It seemed like whenever I thought I couldn't love him any more, the feeling only grew stronger. It hurt, how much I loved him. I melted into his touch and his kiss. He gently lowered me back onto the desk, his hands squeezing my thighs. I grew hard for him, the light fabric of my trousers barely doing anything to conceal my arousal. I threw my arms around his neck, pulling him closer, wanting more. The kiss was magic. Air to starved lungs, water to a parched throat. It fed me. Our tongues explored each other's mouths, circling and teasing and touching. He pushed his crotch up against me, and I felt his bulge rub against mine through our trousers. I pushed my hand down between us and grabbed a handful of his hardness, begging him with my eyes to take me. He eased up, undoing his belt. I turned around, my stomach flat on the desk with my ass pushed out, ready for a punishment. I dropped my trousers to my ankles. Arthur caressed me, and I gasped in surprise as I felt the warm approach of his tongue on my balls, circling them from behind, moving up to greet my hole. I gripped the desk in an attempt to hold on as his tongue made steady motions around my entrance. *It felt so good.*

Then, he reached around and took hold of my cock and began to stroke me. The combination of the two drove me wild, sending me into a frenzy of pleasure. I covered my mouth to suppress a moan, but it fought its way out between my fingers. My cock dripped precome, slicking his hand.

"Fuck me," I said. "Stop teasing me."

Arthur left a final kiss on my ass cheek and stood up, taking position behind me. He gripped my waist with a tight fist. My eyes widened as he entered in one quick motion. I gasped. The desk groaned. He pushed in harder and faster, not wasting time with a gradual crescendo. I held on for dear life, my arms spread and fingers gripping the lip of the desktop as he pounded into me, the swollen curve of his cock hitting me in all the right places.

. . .

I was sure that someone would hear us, that one of the house staff would come in to make sure everything was alright. With every thrust, the desk scraped forward slightly, honking across the wooden floor. If it wasn't so fucking *hot,* I might've found it funny and laughed, but I was too wrapped up in the pure pleasure of being taken by him. He filled me up perfectly, like two puzzle pieces made for one another. Only he could get me this way. Only he could give me this.

"Arthur!" I moaned. His laptop slipped off the desk and clattered to the floor. He ignored it.

I was near the breaking point, just clinging on. I looked over my shoulder at him, and he gazed down at me with those gleaming ruby alpha's eyes and gritted teeth, and he whispered that he was going to come.

We hit the edge at the same time. I felt his cock swell up inside of me just as the orgasm took me. Fireworks exploded in my head and pleasure arced through every muscle of my body. For a moment, I felt like a rag doll, unable to move from the intensity of it. I felt him pulsing inside of me, his warmth filling me up. Slowly, he withdrew. I lay draped over the desk, gasping for breath. Arthur leaned against the desk to catch his breath and it slid forward, dropping him straight down onto his ass. We both started laughing, one of those nonsensical laughs like we both didn't know what was so funny, but still found it to be the most hilarious thing in the world. He held on to my leg, now almost sobbing with laughter. He kissed my thigh.

. . .

"Ahh... We made a mess," he said, through chuckles.

"I think you might need a new computer," I said, and we had another fit.

* * *

Arthur's bike whipped through the track at top speed like a blue streak of lightning. He was determined to break his time record, and this was his twentieth time around the track. He'd been at it for hours without any rest. I'd tried to convince him to stop, but he was dogged in his insistence to keep going, to keep racing.

"You're not going to improve if you're running on fumes," I said into the microphone.

"Just a little more. Just a little quicker. If I just... Just watch my turns. Are you checking them? I *know* I can make it faster."

"You need a break, Arthur," I repeated, calmly. "You need a break, or else you're going to make a mistake. If you crash your bike, it'll be over before it's even begun."

Silence over the channel, and then finally, "Alright. I'll pull in after this lap."

. . .

Trails of vapor and waves of heated air rippled out from the bike's engine compartment as he came to a stop by the monitoring station, and when he stepped out of the bike I could see how exhausted he was. His fur was matted and dull, and his legs quivered for a moment before he caught his balance. He shifted back to human form, and I ran forward and caught his arm over my shoulder to steady him.

"Hounds of Hell, Arthur," I said, and helped him to a seat. "You can't race in this condition."

"I have to," he breathed. I poured some water onto a towel and wiped his forehead and neck with it. He looked out of it. His mind was back in that bike, still on the track.

"You weren't killing yourself like this before," I said. "You were doing excellently."

"I have to," he repeated. "I'm not fast enough yet."

"Arthur." I squeezed his wrist, and he looked at me.

"I know I'm not fast enough yet, Perry. I watched the recordings of Gregor's championship runs. He's a beast."

So that was what this was about. "He's good," I said, nodding. "But I think you're overestimating him."

. . .

"I watched him," he said. "It's pretty clear what his skills are."

"And put up against him, you could match those skills. I know you can."

He shook his head, sweat dripping down his cheeks. I dabbed the damp towel on his face again, and then kissed the side of his forehead.

"I would never have agreed to let you go through with this if I didn't think you'd have a chance," I said. "I've been helping you train these past few days. I've watched you race hundreds of times, now. You can do it. You can beat him. But you need to take a break."

He sighed and slumped into the chair. "You're right, Perry," he said. "I'm just going to make a mistake if I keep this up."

I put my arm around his shoulder, and he rested his head onto mine.

What would happen if he lost? The main thing of course would be that Jupiter and I would still be bound to Gregor. We'd have no choice but to return to Elclaw, and our status in the eyes of the Silver Sun Clan and Gregor's family would be lower than ever. That wasn't a problem for me, I was already treated like dog shit, but for Jupiter...

There was a lot at risk here. It wasn't just our love that was on the line. Arthur and I hadn't really brought up the risks, because we both knew what was at stake and both knew that it was worth it.

"You'll win," I told him. "I'm behind you. Your family is behind you. I know you can do it."

Arthur's cell phone rang, and he pulled it out of his bag. It was his brother, Christophe.

"Hello?" he answered. "I'm at the track." There was a pause, and his eyes narrowed. "I see. Good. It's about damn time. We'll be back."

He slipped the phone into his bag and stood up.

"What's going on?" I asked.

"We need to get back to the house. Christophe has just received word through the clan that Gregor is in Wolfheart, and he's on his way to the Crescent Moon headquarters."

. . .

I stood up, my heart pounding with excitement. "It's about damn time," I said. Arthur smirked and took my hand, and we hurried out to the lot where his motorcycle was parked.

To my surprise, the entire Luna family was gathered at the house, waiting for us. Christophe had made the call to everyone, and they'd all showed up to come with us to the headquarters.

"You didn't all need to come," Arthur said.

"This is a family matter," Loch said. "I'm gonna be there to support my big brother."

"Yeah," Vander said. "Not to mention, intimidate the hell out of Gregor. If he's facing you, he's facing the entire Luna family."

There was an echo of agreement from everyone else. A chill went through my body, and I bit back tears. "You all are wonderful," I said. "To be so supportive of us... Thank you all so much."

"Love is special," said Mason, and Christophe nodded next to him. "Family aside, I think each one of us here understands the significance of its power. We all would do the same in Arthur's position. And we've all been fortunate to have found our loves. So we're going to do everything we can to make sure you two will be together."

"Trust me," Vander said. "We're behind you *all* the way. Even if Arthur loses."

"Thanks for having faith in me," Arthur laughed.

"What Vander means," said Pell, "is that we'll keep fighting for you, no matter the outcome of this race."

"I don't intend to burden you any further than this challenge," Arthur said. "I'm going to win this. It'll be settled, once and for all." He looked confident. It was obvious that the support of his family had lifted him up. The energy of care and determination was palpable in the air. You could see it flickering in the eyes of every one of them, even the children. This was family spirit.

"That's what I like to hear," his father said, and spoke in a booming voice, "Where does a wolf of strength and honor tread?"

"Beneath the crescent moon," everyone replied in unison, their voices reverberating through the room.

. . .

I looked to Arthur, and he smiled at me. "The words of our clan. Soon to be your clan, too."

The family piled into a caravan of cars, and we drove back into downtown Wolfheart to the clan's headquarters, where Jupiter and I would be having our unhappy reunion with Gregor. I was nervous, but more than that I was brimming with a kind of eager determination. With the Luna family around me—my family—it felt like going to battle alongside the strongest, most competent fighters by my side. A legendary team of heroes. No one was going to let anyone down. Everyone would support each other to the last. Gregor didn't have that. The Houndfang family was wealthy and powerful, but this kind of support, this kind of *love*, was non-existent.

The Crescent Moon skyscraper was decorated with fluttering flags bearing the clan's crest, a white sickle of moon over a deep blue backdrop. I was surprised by the formality of our welcoming and the commotion it caused inside the building. As we walked through, guided by a security detail, dozens of workers emerged from offices to get a glimpse of the Luna family in person, the family who had led the Crescent Moon clan for generations. Even as a highborn, this was hardly a typical experience, and I hadn't been prepared for it. Arthur took my hand, and Jupiter clung to my leg, her eyes wide as she took in the hubbub.

We took two elevators up to a floor reserved for family business, and were guided to a conference room.

. . .

"Two of your party is waiting for you inside," the security officer told us, and opened the door. I was shocked to see my brother and none other than my father sitting at the table inside.

"I hope you won't be upset," Dimitrius said, coming up to me. "I asked him to be here. I thought it'd be important."

"Dad," I said.

"Perichor." He gave me a hug, and then crouched down to greet Jupiter. "My little granddaughter."

"Hi, Grandpa," Jupiter said, giving him a hug.

"I know I've been ineffective in aiding you all these years, Perichor," he said to me. "And I understand the anger you have towards me. I live with the decision to bind you to Gregor Houndfang every day, the decision not to challenge your mother on it. I was afraid—am afraid. It's a trait I'm not proud of. But I'm proud of you. There's no fear in you. No hesitation to do what's right for your family. You're a better father than I am."

"You're right," I said. "I don't know if I'll be able to forgive you for the lack of support you've shown me. But... I am glad that you're here. Surprisingly."

. . .

And it was true—I felt an unexpected lightness seeing my father here, knowing that he was on my side.

A man entered and whispered to Christophe, who nodded and spoke up. "Gregor is on his way up."

Arthur and I sat at the conference table, with one seat for my husband on the opposite side, our family lined up behind us. The room fell into silence as we waited. I closed my eyes, and could hear the pounding of my heart. I didn't want to see him again. I'd only been away for a little over a week, but all this time spent with Arthur had made it feel like much longer. I wanted to just continue on like this, to let him disappear as a distant memory, a bad dream. I didn't want to go back to that time, that frame of mind.

I felt Arthur's hand on my thigh, and he gave me a reassuring squeeze. I slipped my hand into his and squeezed back.

He's here with me, I thought. *Everything will be fine.* Immediately, I felt stronger.

There was a knock on the door, and one of the attending security guards announced, "Mr. Gregor Houndfang, Silver Sun Clan," before pulling the doors open.

Two men entered first, Gregor's private security guards, Max and Bingo, two musclebound omegas who I was positive

Gregor had slept with. He didn't make secrets of his trysts, often times on purpose just so I knew. Behind them followed my husband. He looked down his nose at me, glaring with venom in his eyes. Then he found Jupiter, and his expression changed into one of false joy. It was disturbing how easily he could do that, to make himself look so charming when he wanted something.

"Jupiter, little sweetie-pup. Come to your father."

Jupiter stood next to Dimitrius, who had his hand placed gently on his shoulder. She didn't move.

"Come on, Jupiter. You must've missed being kept away from me by your daddy. Isn't he mean? Come here."

"Jupiter?" I called to her, turning around. "Do you want to go to your father? It's your choice."

She shook her head vigorously, backing up further behind Dad and Dimitrius's legs.

"*Dog shit!*" Gregor snapped. "She's been brainwashed by him!" He jabbed a finger at me, and I felt Arthur's grip tighten on my hand.

. . .

"The girl made her own decision," Christophe said, his voice filling the room. It startled me, hearing him speak in such an authoritative tone. It wasn't the same voice that I'd heard during the family conversations at the house, it sounded more like his father's voice. "Take a seat, Mr. Houndfang."

Gregor looked stunned, and it seemed like he was going to carry on, but then decided it would be better not to with the entire Luna family staring him down from across the room. He sat down across from us, and resumed his venomous glare at me. I glared back, feeling strong.

"You've had time to consider the challenge made by Arthur Luna," Christophe said. "A wolf-cycle race, when if defeated, you must nullify your marriage to Perichor. How do you respond to the challenge?"

"Unacceptable," he said. "I lose, I lose everything. I win, what do I get? He's my husband, he's running off and being unfaithful, I shouldn't be defending anything."

I snorted. "I have been faithful for the last thirteen years! Thirteen years that you have, without even any regard for discretion or consideration for the feelings of our daughter, cheated on me!"

"You do understand the consequences of rejecting this challenge of honor, Mr. Houndfang?" Christophe asked, using his tone to silence both sides. "An unwillingness to defend your name will mean the reason for the challenge is justified and the allegations against you are true. Your clan will know. If you do lose the challenge, you will have defended your reputation."

Gregor shifted in his seat. "Yes," he said, unhappily. "Though, I think it's pretty plain to see that the stakes are uneven. I have far more to lose."

"Regardless of how you feel, the challenge stands," Arthur said. "And is bound by the clans. But if it'll make you feel any better, I'll add two things to my offer. If I lose, I'll quit wolf-cycle racing."

I looked at him, surprised.

"And..." He squeezed my hand slightly. "I will exile myself from the Crescent Moon Clan."

A gasp went up from the whole family.

"Arthur," I said, completely shocked. "No!"

"You can't, son," his father said. "You can't do that."

. . .

"I want to make sure that this deal is fairly agreed upon," he said. "As much as I hate admitting it, he's right. There's far more at stake on his side... regardless of his actual feelings towards Perry and Jupiter."

It made me so angry that Gregor had even made this an issue. This was how little he cared about us. He only saw us as property. That was our value to him. Of *course* he wouldn't just care about winning this. There had to be something in it for him other than defending his right to his husband and daughter. *Dog shit!*

"Think about this, Arthur," Christophe said in a low voice.

He nodded. "I've given it plenty of thought."

"Well, I accept those terms," Gregor said, clapping his hands together. "And to be nice, why don't we have the race here, in Wolfheart? Wonderful track you have here. I wouldn't want to have you complaining that you weren't used to the track when I defeat you."

"How thoughtful of you," Arthur said. "Hopefully we won't hear you complaining that I had the home field advantage when you lose."

The clan official who had been witnessing the agreement completed the challenge contract and passed it to Arthur and

Gregor to sign. The silence in the room when Arthur put his pen to the paper was sharp as a knife. It was like every one of the Luna family had held their breath. If Arthur left the clan, it was almost like leaving the family, the two were so intricately intertwined. Even though I understood Arthur's reason for making the decision, I felt horrible about it. I hoped that the Lunas didn't now regret their decision to help me, now that he'd done this.

Gregor signed his name. "You both will be back where you belong soon," he said, standing. "They're *my* husband and daughter. This foolishness will be over and done with soon."

"Don't kid yourself," said Tresten. "Like we'd let anything happen to Perry and Jupiter."

"That's right," Mason said. "You have no idea who you're fucking with."

Gregor fumed, his face twitching. He straightened his jacket, and then smiled. Again, that unsettlingly fast transition of expression. "I'll see you soon, sweetie-pup," he said to Jupiter, and then he strode out the door, his men following behind.

"What a horrible person," Stella said.

. . .

"I'll never get why you and Mom thought he would be a good match for Perry," Dimitrius said to Dad. "Was it seriously just for the status? You'd do that to your son?"

Dad shrunk down. "We didn't know. We interviewed him, and he was always, well, charming. Kind. Honorable. Even as a boy. I'm sorry. I'm sorry."

"I can't believe you," Dimitrius said. "Hounds of hell, Dad."

Basch turned to Dimitrius. "Young man, that's your *father*."

"No, no. He's right," Dad said. "I failed to protect my son. I have to live with that."

"Enough," I said. "It's in the past. And Dad is right. Gregor can be a very likeable person in order to get what he wants. Let's just worry about this challenge."

"That's right," Christophe said. "There's three days until the race. We need to use all our energy to support Arthur and Perry. We're family. We're all together in this."

Jupiter ran over to me, and I picked her up and hugged her close. Arthur and I exchanged a glance, and I could see the simmering anger in his eyes.

. . .

"Thank you," he said. "It makes a big difference to have you all lending your confidence. I know the decision I made was a severe one, but I believe it was important to do. No one will question the fairness of this whole thing when I kick Gregor's ass."

"We understand," Basch said. "It was the honorable thing to do, and we're proud of you."

"We're with you, brother," Loch said, gripping his shoulder. "All the way."

ARTHUR

I stood to the side and watched Perry as he tucked Jupiter into bed. He knelt at her bedside, the warm light of the side table lamp glowing off his face. He pulled the covers up to her chin and kissed her on the cheek.

"Goodnight, sweetie," he said.

"Goodnight, Daddy." She turned and smiled at me. "Goodnight, Arthur."

I crouched next to her. "Goodnight, Jupiter." She reached out and hugged me around my neck, and then kissed me on the cheek. I was stunned for a second; it was the first time she'd ever done anything like that.

"I love you," she said.

. . .

I smiled, and gave her a kiss on her forehead. "I love you too, Jupiter," I said, and Perry rubbed my back. I couldn't help but be moved by Jupiter's tenderness.

"Isn't there something else you wanted to say, sweetie?" Perry asked her.

Jupiter pulled the covers up to her forehead and shook her head.

"Are you sure? I thought you told me there was."

"It's too scary!" she said from underneath the covers, and I laughed.

"What! Too scary?"

"Would you like me to tell Arthur for you?" Perry asked, and she shook her head again. "Well, come on. You should tell him, then. It'll make him happy."

Slowly, she lowered the covers back down to her chin and looked at me with shy eyes. "I hope you win the race," she said hesitantly, and then with decided commitment added, "I want you to be my Papa!"

. . .

My jaw dropped, and I scooped her up into a tight hug. "Thank you, Jupiter. It means a lot to hear you say that. No matter what happens, know that I'll be here for you. And I'm going to do everything I can to make sure that you, your daddy, and I will be together. Okay?"

"Okay," she said, and settled into her pillow. She looked content, and I pulled the covers back up to her chin.

"Get some sleep," I said, and we turned the light off and left her room.

Perry wrapped his arms around me, hugging me from the back. He nuzzled and kissed my neck, and I placed my hand on top of where his forearms crossed my chest. It felt so comforting to feel the movement of his breathing against my back, and the warmth and weight of his body on mine.

I'll never get tired of this feeling, I promised myself. What could be better than feeling his affection for me like that? Feeling the tight squeeze of his arms around me, holding me so close, pulling me in as tight as possible, like he was afraid to let me get away. It was intoxicating. It was everything. How could I live without this? I'd sacrifice everything to always have this.

He kissed my hair and rested his chin into the nape of my neck. His stubble tickled me, and I laughed.

. . .

"That was sweet," he said. I closed my eyes, enjoying the feeling of the vibrato of his voice being absorbed into my back.

"It really was," I agreed.

"She really loves you a lot. I think this is the first time she's felt like she has someone else she can count on. Someone in her corner."

"I love her too," I said, and I felt tears coming to my eyes. "I meant every word. I'm not going to let her down."

Perry's arms released, and I turned around to face him, wrapping my arms around his waist. I hugged him tightly to my chest, his head on my shoulder. He sighed, and I felt the warmth of his breath through my shirt. All vivid, wonderful, precious reminders that he was here with me. That we were together. What a beautiful thing! Not only to have been brought back together, but to have been fortunate enough to even exist at the same time in the first place. Now I couldn't stop the tears from flowing down my cheeks. We stood in silence, just holding one another. Perry took my face into his hands, and he brought his lips to my forehead, then the tip of my nose, and finally to beneath both of my eyes, kissing away my tears.

. . .

"I'll never be able to thank you enough for what you've done—what you're doing—for me." He kissed me, and I savored the taste of his lips on mine. It felt like this was everything I needed to live. I could survive on this moment; on his kiss and his touch.

"And I'll never be able to thank you enough for what you've given me," I said.

"What's that?"

"Love. I'd thought I'd never feel it ever again. But being with you and Jupiter, I feel alive again. Like my life has a purpose. Real purpose."

"Well, that's another thing I have to thank you for," he laughed. "I feel the same way."

We reclined onto my bed, with Perry sat up against the pillows. I laid my head into his lap, and he played with my hair, combing his fingers through it. I closed my eyes, relaxing into the moment. He rubbed his thumbs along my eyebrows and gently down the bridge of my nose. If I had my tail out, it would've been wagging hard. I sighed contently as he returned his fingertips to the top of my head, lightly rubbing them against my scalp. I felt like I was floating in a dream. Perry's scent surrounded me and the warmth of his legs cradled my head and neck, enveloping me in a cocoon of comfort and happiness.

. . .

"There's something that I want to tell you," Perry said. "But..."

"Tell me," I said, opening my eyes. He looked down at me and shook his head.

"I can't."

"What? Why not?"

He looked embarrassed. "Too scary," he said, and laughed.

I laughed with him. "Tell me." He grinned and covered my ears with his hands. His soft palms were warm against my cool earlobes. His mouth moved, and I pulled his hands away. "Hey. I want to be able to hear what you're telling me."

"Too late," he said. "You missed it."

I growled and reached back to tickle his sides. "Come on, spit it out." He grabbed my hands and locked them down at his thighs. He gazed down at me, smiling apologetically.

"I'll tell you later. When I'm ready."

. . .

"Why'd you mention it if you're not ready to tell me?"

He shrugged. "To give you something to look forward to for later."

I laughed and wrestled free from his grip, and twisted onto my knees to face him. "Damn you," I said, and pounced on him, pinning him back into the pillows. He laughed and wrestled against me as I nipped at his neck. I slid my hands around his waist and squeezed him tightly. He wriggled and kicked his legs, and tried to tickle my waist. "Tell me, tell me," I murmured into his neck.

"Later," he cackled as I licked his earlobe. He wrapped his thighs around my waist and in one quick motion, twisted me onto my back so that he was on top. "Okay?" he said, smiling down at me.

"Fine, if you insist." I slid my hand around the back of his neck and gently pulled his face down to me. We kissed, and he relaxed against me, resting his head on my chest. I held him against me, his head rising and falling with each breath. Everything felt so perfect. I didn't want to move from that position. I wanted to preserve the moment forever.

We stayed like that until we fell asleep, and drifted off into our dreams together.

* * *

"The White Tree Track called to confirm the race," Christophe told me the following day. "Everything is set."

"Good." I nodded. "Excellent."

"You look nervous."

I huffed. "No shit. The pressure is on."

"I've got another piece of news that might make you happy."

"What's that?"

He straightened his shirt in an attempt to look dramatic. "I also got a call today from the head of the White Tree Clan. The news is traveling through the pipeline. In support of your cause, they've offered to grant you exclusive after-hours practice time at the track."

My mouth dropped open. "Hounds of Hell. That does make me happy."

I'd been practicing my ass off at the abandoned track, which was out of standard, in disrepair, and was missing several of the standard obstacles that were at White Tree—ones that Gregor would've had tons of experience with from his home track. I'd told myself I'd make do with what I had, but it'd always been at the back of my mind. Without the ability to practice on a true championship track, I'd be at a great disadvantage.

Until now.

"And," Christophe said, "We've been reached out to by the Birch Mountain Clan. They own Ripclaw Performance, and have offered to sponsor maintenance of your bike. The Crescent Moon's allies are behind you, Arthur. The word is getting out."

I went outside to tell Perry. He was playing with Jupiter, the both of them in their wolf forms, chasing each other around in the forest that bordered the property. I leaned against a tree and watched them, enjoying seeing their happiness. Jupiter looked so carefree, the way she bounded and pranced around, enjoying her new ability. Her ears pricked up and she sniffed the air and then looked at me.

"Arthur!" she barked, hopping excitedly into the air. She sprinted at me, her tongue lolling out the side of her muzzle, and jumped into my arms. Shifter pups weren't exactly small, and she knocked me back onto my butt. "Come and play?" she asked, licking my face.

"Okay, okay," I said, laughing. Everything else in my head seemed to lose its importance at that moment. I just wanted to make Jupiter happy, to enjoy her laughter. I shifted into my wolf form and ran after her.

"Welcome," Perry said. "She's roped you in."

"So, what are we playing?"

"Chase," she said, hopping back and forth from forepaw to rear paw like a bucking horse. Then she took off into the trees, her ears flopping wildly as she ran.

"We'd better get her," I said to Perry, and the two of us sprinted after her, making sure to stay just behind her. I growled playfully and leapt at her, purposefully sailing over her and rolling across the ground. She giggled, ran up to me, and tugged at my tail with her teeth.

"I'm gonna catch you!" Perry barked, and he pounced at her. She yelped and bolted away, twisting around the trees. Perry followed after, laughing as she evaded him. I got up and ran to catch up, ducking back and forth to avoid the trees.

Perry nipped at the end of Jupiter's tail, and she shrieked and galloped faster. I charged ahead and yanked her up by the scruff of her neck, tossing her up into the air. I shifted back to my human form, and caught her as she fell.

. . .

"Got ya," I said. She giggled and shifted back to human form and hugged me around my neck. Perry shifted back too, and mussed up Jupiter's hair.

"You're getting used to your legs pretty quick. Aren't you, sweetie?"

"It's fun to run with them," she said. "I can run fast."

"You sure can," I said. "And you'll only get faster." I set her down, and she squeezed her arms around my leg and stood on my shoe.

"Run with me again, Papa?" she said. I blinked, surprised.

"Ah..."

"Arthur isn't your Papa yet, sweetie," Perry said gently.

"Why not?"

"Because he needs to win his race in order for us to be able to move here for good. Once that happens, then he'll be your Papa."

. . .

"What if he loses?" she asked, squeezing my leg tighter.

"I won't," I said, petting her head.

"I want you to be Papa now anyway," she said.

"Jupiter..."

"That's alright," I said. "Do you want to call me Papa? Will that make you happy?" She looked up at me and nodded, and I crouched down to her level, taking her two little hands in mine. "Then you can call me Papa. I don't mind. And I want you to remember that no matter what happens, you can always think of me as Papa. Okay?"

"Okay."

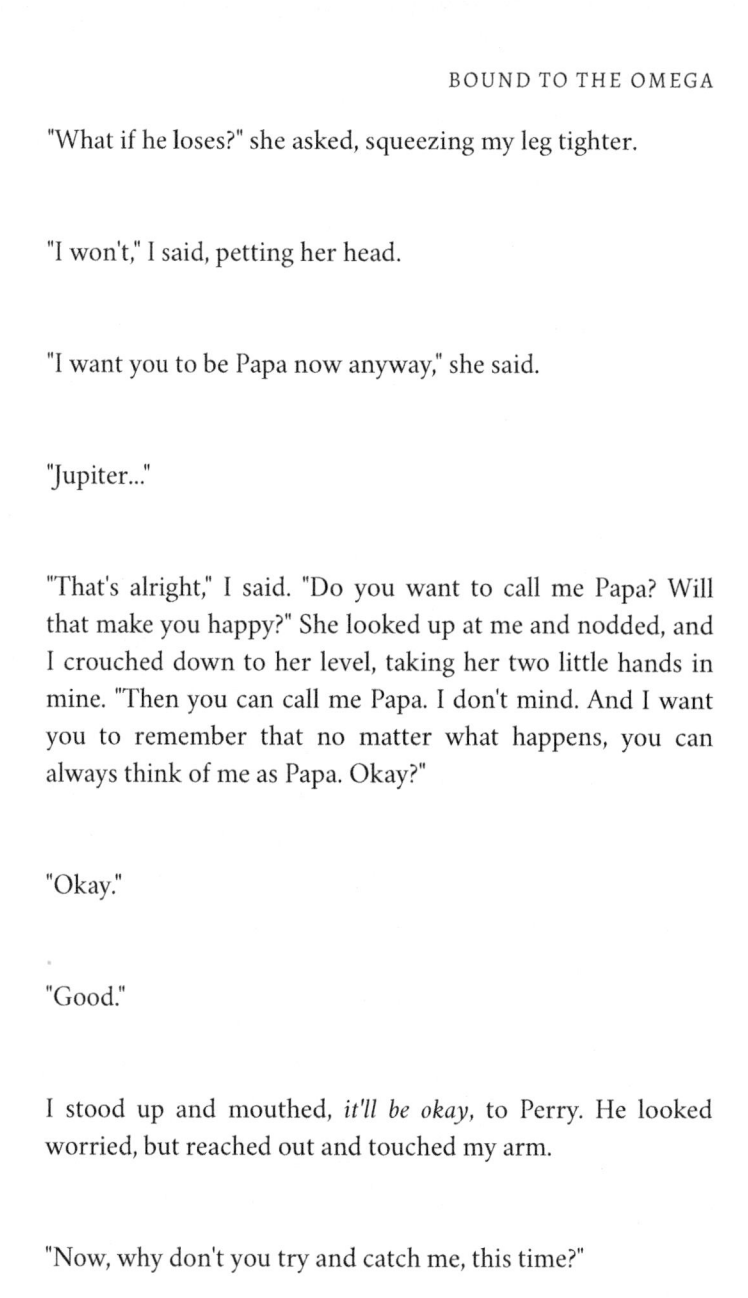

"Good."

I stood up and mouthed, *it'll be okay*, to Perry. He looked worried, but reached out and touched my arm.

"Now, why don't you try and catch me, this time?"

Jupiter grinned. "Okay!"

. . .

"Let's go, Perry. Try and catch me."

I turned and sprinted away, shifting mid-step. Jupiter squealed and followed, with Perry close behind.

That evening, Perry and I went to the White Tree Track for the first night of training and practice there. We pulled up to the front of the gigantic, glimmering arena, and I realized that neither of us had been back here since the day this all started. It'd been Kota's Teller ceremony, a day meant for good fortune and fate. It seemed like some of that fate altering magic had been passed to me. I took his hand, and the two of us stood in a silent reverence for a moment, both of us contemplating what had brought us here, and brought us back together.

"Amazing, isn't it?" he asked. "I don't know if I'll ever be able to stop asking myself what would have happened if things had gone just a little differently that day. If I hadn't seen you."

"Nothing," I said. "Because I would've found you again anyway. Loch knew that you were back in town. He told me that day. He'd heard it from Dimitrius."

"Really?"

. . .

"Yeah. I definitely didn't expect to see you at the track. I didn't expect to see you that day. But you were on my mind, and I was planning on showing up at your family home to see if you were there. So, no matter what, fate meant for us to meet again."

"I didn't know that," he said. "You're right. I guess we had no choice in the matter, huh?"

"Nope. But I'm not going to get complacent, thinking that fate is on our side. I know what Gregor can do on that track."

Inside, we were greeted by one of the track managers, who showed us down to the garages. The arena was spectacularly impressive during its operating hours, filled with the noise of a stadium filled with people and the roar of the bikes, but it took an equally awe-inspiring state when it was empty. Workers picked through the stands, cleaning them, but otherwise we were the only people inside. It felt like being alone in a city. Having such silence in so huge a place gave it a mystical quality, like the temple that was not too far away.

"We have a database of records of the races run here," the track manager said. "If you wish, you can pull them up and run time trials against ghosts. The arena's system will network with your bike, and display a ghost racer of whoever you want to try running against."

"What does that mean?" Perry asked him.

. . .

"It means that Mr. Luna can practice against Gregor Houndfang's previous races," the manager said with a slim smile, obviously proud of his cutting-edge system.

I searched through the computer and found Gregor's records. I'd seen them before, but I still felt nervous looking at them. He was fast. Damn fast. He was a pro. I called up the race that I'd studied on my computer, and locked it into the track's system.

"Now what?" I asked the manager.

"Go to your bike," he said.

Perry took up his position at the monitor, and I jogged out to the track, dropping to my paws as my body shifted into wolf form. I drew in a deep breath, pre-visualizing what the race night would be like. The house would likely be packed. It wasn't a publicized event, but people knew who we were, and it was apparent that the reason for the challenge was spreading quickly by word of mouth. I smelled the lingering pang of burnt rubber and gasoline from today's races, and I could almost hear the roar of a crowd. Excitement coursed through my body. I was going to push my skills to the very edge. I was going to get better. And in two days, I was going to win.

. . .

I climbed into the cockpit of my bike and sealed the door, shrouding me in momentary darkness until the bike's electronics activated and the window illuminated with the heads-up display information. I locked my paws into the control ports, and lit up the engine. The bike shook to life, like a creature waking from an angry sleep.

"Monitor's up," Perry said, through the radio. "This is crazy."

"What is?" I asked.

"This is my first time doing this on a proper system. Everything is so much more... overwhelming. And it literally looks like there's another bike on the track with you."

I looked to my right, and was surprised to see a shimmering, spectral looking bike waiting next to mine. It was the training system that the manager had mentioned. Despite all the years I'd raced at White Tree, I'd never had a chance to use something like this before. This was going to vastly improve my skill level. I could actually study Gregor's driving style *up close*, as if he were really on the track with me.

"Ready?" Perry asked.

The bike's systems flashed green: all safety and system checks completed. "Ready," I said.

. . .

"Countdown. On your marks."

The lights above the track flashed red, then yellow, and finally... green. I opened the throttle and shot forward like a missile, the arena around me streaking into a blur. For a moment, I was startled by the grip I had on the track, like my bike was latched onto the asphalt with glue. I'd gotten used to practicing at the abandoned proving grounds, riding on unmaintained track that made my bike feel like it was going to spin out at any moment. But that was a good thing. I'd done so many practice races there that I'd developed a much more delicate sense of control because of it.

I looked to my right and saw the ghost bike flying along right at my side. *Come on,* I thought. *Let's do this.*

By the end of the practice run, I was panting to catch my breath. My body shook with adrenaline, and I stumbled out of the cockpit onto wobbly legs. I'd expected the first run to not be so great, but I hadn't expected to get my tail kicked so fucking thoroughly. I'd kept up with Gregor's ghost run for the first half, even pulling ahead of him several times, but as soon as we entered into the major obstacles--the ones that the abandoned track didn't have—I completely fell behind, to the point where catching up was just a dream.

Perry ran over to me, and I collapsed onto the ground. "Are you okay?" he asked. "Shift back. Cool down."

. . .

"No," I grunted. "It's just the first run. Just some water."

He looked like he wanted to argue, but he knew I was right. Time was really precious now. There'd be little room for rest this time.

I lapped up water from a watering station in the pit, and then trotted back to my bike, sealing the door behind me. I fired up the engine, settled into the controls, and narrowed my eyes on the track. *Again.*

"Watch your speed when entering The Dog's Eye," Perry said. "Don't rush it. If you rush it, you'll end up losing time trying to correct for small mistakes."

"Right," I growled. "Let's do this."

PERRY

We were at a clear disadvantage, I knew that. Not only did Arthur have less practice time here, he didn't have a professional, dedicated track guide watching the monitors for him. All he had was me: someone who knew a thing or two about wolf-cycle racing, but was definitely no professional. He was counting on me to help him improve his runs, and we both had to trust that my observations and advice were actually doing that.

"Increase by five on the upcoming corner," I said, wiping a gallon of sweat from my forehead. Being here on this track, knowing the challenge was really happening in just a couple days... There was real pressure now, pressure that I hadn't felt before. "Wait, decrease by five," I said, quickly. "Take it hard."

His voice gurgled through the radio. "Shit."

. . .

"I'm sorry," I said. I swallowed a lump in my throat and switched monitor views so that I could see the track from the top down. He banked hard into the corner right alongside Gregor's ghost, and pulled out of it slightly ahead. I breathed out in relief. "You came out ahead. Alright. Great."

"You okay?" he asked. I hit a button on the console, and a picture in picture display of inside his cockpit appeared on the monitor. His eyes were fixed and focused, his ears flattened back against his head. He looked far more relaxed than I felt. It was our sixth time through the course, and Arthur had only finished ahead once.

"Fine," I said, wiping away another torrent of sweat from my forehead with the back of my hand.

"You sound nervous," he said. "I can't have you being nervous. What's the matter?"

"Nervous? What are you talking about?" I squeaked out a nervous laugh, and then coughed it away.

"Perry..." His eyes flicked up to the camera for a half a second.

"Enter the next straightaway at open throttle," I said. "Release halfway through, and then decrease speed. Don't worry about me, Arthur. I'm managing over here."

. . .

His bike rocketed into the straightaway, increasing speed. On the monitor, his eyes narrowed into an intense grimace. He was still just even with the ghost bike, and never able to pull too far ahead, but also never falling too far behind. It was a constant stalemate, but that was a problem. He was just barely holding on to his position. One screw-up and it was over. It seemed like the chance of a win or loss was split down the middle, with the scaled teetering against him.

"I... need you... to not just... manage..." The force of accelerating into the straightaway made it hard to speak. His fur matted back, making it look like a fan was blowing in his face. Halfway into the straightaway, both he and the ghost eased off their throttles and then changed gears, cutting their speed. They curved into the turn at the end like two synchronized dancers. They zipped along The Walls like two mirror images of one another, and then entered the final straightaway before The Forest.

"I can't do this without your help," he said. "The only way I'm going to be able to get through this course ahead of Gregor is with you."

"I know," I said. "But that's what I'm worried about. Maybe we should hire a real track guide. Someone who really knows what they're doing."

"I need *you*," Arthur said. "Nobody else can do this except for you. You know why? Because we're connected. We've got something no one else has."

. . .

Of course.

He was right. I had to trust our connection, our love. He trusted it. He trusted me.

"Okay," I said. The overwhelming nervous feeling was subsiding. I was in control again. I nodded to myself and tapped the buttons on the control panel, bringing up readouts on both Arthur and Gregor's acceleration and brake pressure. "Final stretch. Let's beat that ghost."

"Alright," he said, a grin spreading across his muzzle.

"You're going to need to enter The Forest at top speed in order to match Gregor," I told him. "And you'll need to be precise as possible when going around the pylons."

He jammed the accelerator and flew into the obstacle, whizzing by the the gigantic concrete pillars. He was elegant, but Gregor's ghost still had an edge on him. His movements were obviously more economical than Arthur's, wasting absolutely no speed. It was adding up, and Arthur was pulling slightly behind. I could see the frustration in his face as he looked out the side of the cockpit window and saw Gregor ahead of him. His fangs were gritted in a snarl of concentration. On the monitor, I saw that he was opening the throttle, increasing speed.

. . .

"Careful," I said, alarmed. Going faster here wasn't necessarily the best idea. Too fast, and it'd be impossible to avoid clipping one of the pylons.

"Just a bit," he growled.

He'd evened his position again, but I could see that he was at the verge of being out of control.

"Slow down, Arthur," I said. "Slow down."

He kept the throttle open, and zigzagged between the pylons. I gripped the side of the monitor, my heart hammering with growing panic. Was I just afraid for him? Not pushing him hard enough because I didn't want to see him hurt? Or was he really in the danger my gut was telling me he was in?

"Slow down!" I shouted. He had pulled ahead, but...

He arced around a pylon, and it became obvious both to him and I that he was on a collision course with one straight ahead of him. The bike banked but couldn't turn fast enough. He slammed on the brakes, sending white smoke jetting from both his wheels. The bike spun on the track, like a whirligig blown in the wind. Every muscle in my body tensed as I watched him skid towards the pylon, the tires screeching across the asphalt.

"No!"

I watched as the bike stopped just inches away from slamming sideways into the pylon, smoke continuing to billow up from the tires. On the monitor, Arthur sat frozen, his eyes wide. Gregor's ghost disappeared into the distance.

"Shit," he muttered. "Dammit."

Arthur slowly brought the stalled engine back to life and pulled the bike through the rest of obstacle, and into the pit. He stepped out, shifting back to human form. I ran to him and pushed him.

"What the hell, Arthur?" I shouted.

He stumbled back and fell against the side of the wolf-cycle. He looked stunned and ashamed, and I grabbed him and hugged him tightly.

"If you're going to tell me those things, at least *listen* to me," I said. He was trembling slightly in my arms.

. . .

"I'm sorry," he said. "I thought... I wasn't thinking. I saw him pulling ahead of me and saw no other way."

"Dammit, you could've crashed. You know how delicate the balance is in that section. Speed doesn't always help."

"I know," he said, shaking his head. "I'm sorry, Perry."

We walked around the bike to inspect it. There was no visible damage, except that the tires were obviously worn.

"Maybe I could've pulled it off with fresh tires," he said. "Six runs without a tire change. That could be it."

"Or maybe you were just going too fast," I said. "Please don't do that again. You're going to kill me."

We brought the bike back in to the garage. Without a pit crew here, we couldn't change the tires. We'd just reached the limit of our practice for the night, and just as well. We'd both lost track of the time, and the exhaustion was catching up with us. That was how these kinds of mistakes happened...

When we got back to the house, Arthur filled the bathtub and the two of us dipped into it. Arthur wrapped me up in his arms as we sank into the piping hot water, and I felt the tension slowly dissipating from my body. I was surprised to feel him shivering.

"Arthur?" I turned to look at him, and he looked away. "What is it?" I asked.

"I really fucked up," he said. "I keep playing that moment over and over. I feel like an idiot, telling you to help me and then ignoring you like that. It could've been all over. I feel like... Like that was something Gregor would've done."

"No," I said. "Uh-uh." I brushed his hair back from his forehead and kissed him there. "You are in no way like that man. Not at all. Let's just concentrate on what we have to do. How to beat him."

"Yeah," he said, and kissed me. We both sank further down into the tub as I relaxed into his arms. "How to beat him..."

"Maybe... I might have an idea."

"I'm open to any and all ideas."

"We have access to this new system, the ghost system. We've been racing against Gregor's records, trying to improve against his style of racing. Maybe we ought to be looking at other people?"

. . .

"Other people?"

"Other racers. Ones that have totally *destroyed* Gregor on the White Tree track. That way you pick up new techniques, and you see what his weaknesses are."

"Hounds of Hell," he said. "You're absolutely right." He kissed my cheek.

I grinned and tilted my head back to steal another kiss from him. "We make a pretty damn good team, don't we?"

He kissed my neck and my shoulder. "I'll say. I can't even imagine what I'd do without you."

As he kissed me, I felt excitement rushing between my thighs. In the heat of the bathwater, my cock hardened and rose. I let my hand sneak between his legs, and found his length. He smiled and murmured as I pulled on him, and his hand moved down to reciprocate. The water sloshed gently with our movements. The all-enveloping warmth of the bath only increased the pleasure of his strokes, and I moaned softly and pulled him into another kiss. I loved the feeling of his naked skin against me, the slippery curves of his muscles up against my back. Our tongues lolled against one another, teasing and exploring, and the heat emanating from the bath made my head spin.

. . .

"Can I wash you?" Arthur asked.

"Okay," I said, not exactly sure what he meant.

We stood up, and Arthur soaped up a bath sponge. I laughed. "You're literally going to wash me?"

"What did you think I meant?"

"I dunno. Something dirty."

"Calm down," he smiled. "Dirty comes later."

He scrubbed my body with the sponge, and then even shampooed my hair. I closed my eyes, unable not to fall into a state of relaxation as he massaged his fingers through my hair. Then he moved his hands down, massaging the soap into my neck and shoulders. He went down further still, to my arms, and my chest. My cock throbbed expectantly, but he teased me by skirting around the area, moving to my thighs and the rest of my legs. Then he turned the shower on and rinsed the soap off, taking care to wash all of the shampoo from my hair. My eyes still closed, I gasped as I felt a warm sensation play across my nipple. His tongue circled my right one, then my left and then he began to kiss his way down my chest. When he reached my stomach, he took time to kiss each of my abs. He was taking his sweet time getting down to my cock, and he knew it was driving me crazy. He kissed my inner thigh, and then the other, and for a second I considered twisting my hips and slapping him on the side of the head with my cock as punishment for teasing me, but refrained with a private smile.

Then, the tip of his tongue nipped my balls, sending a tingling shiver up through my entire body. I gasped and squirmed, waiting for more, but there was nothing.

"Keep your eyes closed," he said, and I did. A moment later, there was another playful lick on my balls. My cock bounced as I tightened my muscles in surprise. With all the anticipation, I could feel the precome that was beading up at the tip, probably dripping down into the water.

Suddenly, my cock was enveloped in a tight warmth, like being dipped into warm cream. My knees shook and I cried out and reached out to steady myself against the wall. Even with that incredible explosion of pleasure, I kept my eyes shut. I heard the bathwater moving gently, the only evidence of Arthur's movements. Otherwise, it just felt like unexplainable pleasure on my cock. At times, it felt like he was stroking me, other times sucking me. I had no idea what he could be doing to make me feel this good, and I didn't dare open my eyes to ruin the secret. I ran my hand back through my hair, laughing with amazement at how damn good it felt.

. . .

"Arthur, that's so good... Oh shit, keep doing that. Oh *fuck*, I'm going to come soon."

I heard him murmur in response; a happy, encouraging sound. I groaned as the climax hit me, bursting through my mind and my body like the trembling roar of an engine. I tossed my head back as the sensation rolled on, and Arthur continued to pleasure me. My legs trembled and shook, and I had to take a step back to stop myself from getting overwhelmed. I opened my eyes, and Arthur was there on his knees in front of me, licking his lips. Slowly, I lowered myself into the bath. My head spun like I'd just sprinted a mile.

"Hounds of Hell," I sighed, sinking down into the water to my chin. "That was good."

He came forward through the water and kissed me. "Relaxed?" he asked.

"Incredibly," I said. "But not so relaxed that I can't do this." I reached my hand through the water and took hold of his heavy cock, which hung just below the surface. His eyelids drooped sensuously as I stroked him, his lips parting just slightly to let out a contented sigh.

"Ah..."

. . .

I leaned forward and silenced him with a kiss. Then, with his cock still in my grasp, I turned around onto my knees and presented myself to him. I guided him forward, pulling him up to my entrance, and Arthur went the rest of the way himself. He took me by the waist and inched his way forward, pushing into me, inch by inch, until he finally reached the hilt.

"Oh, shit..." he murmured, and then slowly began to move his hips. Back and forth, back and forth. The water in the bathtub rocked with our movements, building momentum as he increased his speed and ferocity until it sloshed up like waves breaking on a wall. I pulled the plug, and the water slowly drained as he fucked me.

The slaps of skin against skin echoed through the tiled bathroom, and hearing those obscene noises only turned me on even more. A small whirlpool formed around the drain. The water level lowered, Arthur went harder. I lowered my head to the floor and pushed my ass up towards him, opening myself up more for his hard length.

He squeezed my ass to signal his nearing climax, and I felt his cock throb deep inside me as he made one final thrust. It continued to pulse with the waves of his orgasm, and the sound of our heavy breaths filled the room. We stayed locked like that for a moment, too taken by the pleasure of it all to even consider moving. Then, slowly, he withdrew from me, and I could feel his overflow spilling out of me, a delicious warmth. I wrapped my arms around his neck and kissed him, grinning as I did.

. . .

"Are you relaxed?" I asked him.

"Absolutely," he breathed.

We collapsed into the covers together, still naked. I nuzzled up to him and he put his arm around me. We both sighed, sleepy and happy, and burrowed deep into those welcoming blankets. I felt like I was glowing with warmth and love, like nothing in the universe could get any better than this. I lay there, feeling the embrace of sleep slowly drawing me in. I felt so safe with him. I remembered that thing that I'd been too nervous to tell him the other day, and gathered my courage. Why was I afraid to say it? It wasn't *that* big a deal, and yet it was.

"Hey," I said, "So that thing I was going to tell you the other day... I want to tell it to you now."

I was met with silence. "Arthur?" I asked, softly. I turned to look at his face and saw that he was asleep, his lips parted slightly as he breathed. He looked so peaceful. I knew how beat he was—we both were. I kissed his lips. They were soft on mine, and they unconsciously returned the kiss. He murmured in his sleep, and I kissed him again before relaxing into the pillow and closing my eyes. Within seconds, I was out.

* * *

I watched Arthur's bike running tandem next to two ghost bikes on the monitors, one belonging to Gregor, the other belonging to a local champion who had consistently come up on top against Gregor every time they'd raced at White Tree. Arthur was still struggling, but he was more determined than ever. And we were right—seeing this new race record was unveiling so many things about Gregor's technique. It was revealing to see how differently Gregor raced when he was up against someone he had a weakness against. It was obvious how fragile he was, how easily he could be shaken when not at the top.

"He just made a mistake," Arthur said. "Did you see that?"

"I did," I replied. "Went too hard on the brake. I can see him. I know exactly what was going through his head at that moment. He was furious about not anticipating the other racer in that turn. He's getting himself all worked up."

"Shit. He's still damn good, though."

I watched as the three bikes swung another hard corner, the new bike hugging the turn sharply and coming in the lead. Arthur pulled out last, just barely behind Gregor's. By the end of the lap, he pulled in neck and neck with him. I jogged over to meet him, and we took a moment to go over the race together, studying the technique of the new racer. Then Arthur went again. This time, we picked a different record from a different racer who had a perfect win record against Gregor.

. . .

I could see him improving. I could tell that a certain pressure that'd been there earlier was gone, now that he was free from Gregor's ghost.

ARTHUR

The day before the race, Perry and I took a walk around the Luna property with Jupiter in the lead, sniffing around the trees and bushes. She was still enjoying the novelty of her wolf form, and it seemed like she was spending more time shifted than not. Perry walked closely by my side, his fingers intertwined with mine. I did what I could to keep my mind present, to enjoy this moment with them. It was hard not to find myself back at the track, analyzing the races in my head. *Do I enter this turn at this angle? Or just slightly less? This speed? Gregor seemed to respond this way...*

"Do you recall the time we first met?" Perry's soft voice called me back from the madness. I looked at him, and he returned an inquisitive glance and began to swing my hand playfully.

"The very first time?" I asked.

. . .

"The very first time."

All thoughts and anxieties of tomorrow melted away as my thoughts drifted back in time. The White Tree Track was at the center of it all.

"I do," I said. It was a memory I'd pushed out of my head for the past thirteen years, along with all the others, so I was surprised how clearly I could recall it now. It filled me with a tingle of nostalgia. "I was in pre-academy," I said, "hardly the same wolf I was today. I was at the White Tree Track watching the races, and I snuck down to the bike bays for a hope at a peek at wolf-cycles. That's when I saw you. I noticed you because you were holding a bag with the Sycamore Creek school logo, and I wanted to know who else at my school was interested in wolf-cycles. I introduced myself to you, and we talked about the bikes."

"Talked?" Perry laughed. "You mean, argued? We disagreed on practically everything! You said the 486z 'Claw' was superior to the 'Vector' model because of its fuel system. Our debate got so heated that we got kicked out of the pits!"

"Okay, you remember this better than I do, apparently," I said, laughing. "I remember having a great conversation with you about the bikes, getting so involved we were asked to leave, and then continuing it all the way back up to the stands."

. . .

"People were annoyed because we were blabbing while the races were going on, yelling over the sound of the engines."

"I remember none of this," I admitted. "I do remember the feeling of wanting to keep talking to you, though. Of really having a lot of fun talking to you."

"You found me the next day at school. I didn't realize you'd seen my bag, I was wondering how this weirdo had found me at my school."

"Really?" I asked.

"Yes! I had no idea."

"But we became friends after that."

"Best friends," he amended. "Couldn't get you away from me."

I smiled, remembering. "It wasn't long before I had a huge crush on you. Huge. I was afraid to ruin our friendship, so I didn't say anything."

"You were just shy," Perry said, poking me in my side. "If I'd had a crush on you at that time, I would've said something."

. . .

"You didn't have a crush on me?" I asked, with feigned shock.

"I grew up with the idea that I already belonged to an alpha. It's odd to think I actually felt proud about it back then. My parents had convinced me it was something to look forward to. I was pretty prissy about it, if I recall..."

I nodded. "You were sort of cold about your feelings. You didn't let people get close to you."

"I guess it was a defense. I knew I was promised to Gregor, so I never gave romance a thought. I always just believed it was something that wouldn't happen for me. What a shock, when I realized I was falling for you."

I nodded, silently. I knew he'd struggled, but it was a story he'd never told me.

"It felt like nothing made sense. How could my parents do this to me? That was all I could think. How could they imprison me like this? I wasn't supposed to fall in love with anyone else. I was supposed to marry Gregor, and I would fall in love with him. The shit I'd imagined about him, what I fantasized it'd be like. It makes me want to throw up. I'd been convinced that *I* was lucky, being arranged to him. I was in denial about it for a while. I didn't want to admit to myself that I could actually be feeling something for you. I considered breaking off our friendship so many times."

. . .

"You tried," I said. "Our last year at Sycamore. You went cold on me, all of a sudden."

"I'm sorry I did that to you," he said, squeezing my hand. "I thought I would be saving myself, when I did that. It was stupid, and selfish. And I realized very quickly that trying to break things off was a lost cause. I was already in deep."

"That whole thing gave me courage," I said. "I realized I shouldn't be afraid of what would happen. I was going to lose you anyway. And almost losing you as a friend, I realized I'd much rather lose you as a lover."

"It gave me courage too," said Perry. "It was a catalyzing moment, wasn't it? And then we both planned to tell each other we were in love on the same day."

I laughed. "Fate has always had a way of fucking with us, I guess."

He stopped and tugged me close to him, wrapping his arms around my waist. "I have something to tell you. Two things, actually."

"Oh?" I kissed him on his forehead. "Is it *the* thing? You aren't afraid anymore?"

. . .

"I'm still afraid. But I'm ready to tell you. Are you ready to hear it?"

"Of course."

He brushed my hair back, and he smiled, his eyes sparkling. Was he crying? I rubbed the corner of his eye with my thumb, curious about what could be making him feel this way.

"I just wanted to say," he announced, straightening the front of my shirt, "that... I love you."

I laughed. "I know that. I love you too."

"And! And, even though Gregor has been my husband for thirteen years... You have *always* been my mate."

My heart caught in my throat. "You know I feel the same way," I said. "Always."

"And the other thing. It's a big one."

"Okay."

. . .

"I'm pregnant."

It took me several seconds to comprehend what Perry had just said to me. *Pregnant?* I was so shocked, the possibility that I might be the father hardly even entered my head, until he said to me, "It's yours."

I stammered, trying to make sense of it. "But, it's only been like, a week. Is it possible?"

He nodded. "I can tell. When I shift, I can sense it. And I know without a doubt that it's yours, because, well... You're the only one it could be."

My head was spinning. "Hounds of Hell," I said, stunned. "We're going to have a baby..."

Perry and I hadn't taken the precaution of protected sex, so it really shouldn't have been a surprise. He was pregnant with my child.

"Are you... okay?" he asked, looking concerned. "I thought it was important to tell you before the race. I didn't want to keep it from you."

. . .

"I'm fine, Perry," I said, shaking away the shock. "I just... We're going to have a baby." I laughed and hugged him. "We're going to have a baby!"

Jupiter pranced over and sat down at our feet, her tail wagging. "Why are you crying, Papa Arthur?" she asked.

"You're going to be a big sister soon," I told her.

Her tail wagged furiously, and she shifted back into human form and jumped up into my arms. Perry laughed and hugged the both of us. I was overwhelmed; it just didn't feel real. We were going to have a baby. Regardless of what happened, Perry and I were bound together. For a brief moment, the whirl of happiness was replaced by a sharp fear. Our situation had become infinitely more complicated. Now, more than ever, I *had* to win that race.

I could see that same glimmer of uncertainty in Perry's eye. "We're going to be okay," I told him. "I'll make sure of it. This baby will be yours and mine, okay? No one will come between our family. No one."

That night, I couldn't sleep. I lay in bed, staring at the ceiling, my thoughts back on the track. Now, the news of my child had joined the thoughts of tomorrow's race. Perry stirred and nuzzled his face into my neck.

. . .

"I can hear you thinking," he said, his voice gravelly with sleep. "Can't fall asleep, huh?"

"I didn't expect I'd be able to," I said. "Tomorrow is the most important day of my life."

"Mine too," he said.

"Our lives," I said.

"No matter what happens tomorrow," he said. "I know we'll find a way to be together. Do you know why? Because we're mates."

I nodded, silently.

"I think I know a way to help us sleep," he said. "It's tried and true."

"How's that?"

In the dark, I felt his soft breath on my neck, and the gentle tickle of his lips. Then, the rustle of the sheets as his hand slipped underneath the waistband of my pajamas.

* * *

I looked out the car window as Stephen drove Perry and I to the White Tree Track. Grey clouds were rolling across the sky, casting the world in a solemn grey haze. I didn't necessarily believe in omens, but it wasn't exactly an uplifting feeling.

"Looks like rain," Perry said. "That wasn't expected."

"No," I said, absently. He touched my leg.

We pulled out of the private access highway into downtown Wolfheart. I saw the impressive dome of the temple off in the distance, and asked Stephen to make a quick detour.

"Making an offering for luck, sir?" he asked.

"I think I'll need all the help I can get," I replied, but there was another reason I wanted to stop there. "We'll just be a couple minutes," I told him as we pulled into the parking lot. "Keep the car running."

"Yes, sir."

Perry and I hurried inside. One of the priests shuffled by, swinging a silver incense holder, the grey-red incense smoke flowing out of the intricate geometry cut into its sides. He stopped and turned towards us. I nodded to him respectfully, and he held up an open palm, and drew his hood to his shoulders. He was half shifted, his face part wolf, part man.

"Arthur Luna and Perry Houndfang," he said in a low voice.

"Master?" I said. I wasn't expecting to be addressed.

He shuffled slowly over to us, his hands clutched at his waist. The incense holder dangled in front of him, giving the impression that he was drifting on a cloud of smoke.

"It is a day of great importance to you both," he said, and Perry and I exchanged a curious glance.

"Yes, it is," Perry said. "How did you know? Have you seen something in our futures?"

The priest chuckled, a low and dry sound. "No," he said. "Your challenge isn't exactly hidden knowledge. Word has been going around. We have a bet going, amongst the priests. I hope you win. Otherwise, I'm going to be out a fair sum of money."

I snorted a laugh. "Well then maybe you can give us a blessing for the race. And another, too."

. . .

After he made an offering for us for the race, he took us to the fertility shrines and assisted us in a prayer for our child. Perry and I shifted into our wolf forms and touched noses to the tree. I closed my eyes, picturing the spark of life that had started to form inside Perry.

For this child, I thought.

PERRY

The stadium was filled beyond the normal turnout for an open race day. The stands were packed with people, and Arthur's name was on their lips. Those who hadn't come because of the challenge were quickly sucked into the excitement by those who had. All sorts of wild rumors were flying around about the nature of the challenge. Arthur had stolen me away from a loving husband. No, Gregor had used me as a betting chip to win the Luna fortune. Or was it a stunt to draw attention to a promising new racer's blossoming career? The stories flew through the stands, each person convinced theirs was accurate, and betting accordingly. It seemed like only a minority knew the actual reason for the challenge, but no one really seemed to care. For most, it was a rare and exciting occasion: A Luna against a popular foreign driver.

The family had a private box overlooking the track, and we went there first. Jupiter was sitting on Dimitrius's lap, and he was pointing down to the track and explaining things to her.

Basch and Stella took turns looking through a set of binoculars, while Kota and Alexis chased each other around the box. Vander, Pell, Christophe, and Mason all stood at the window, watching the races that were currently going on. Loch and Tresten sat on one of the leather couches and looked over a betting tablet. Jupiter was the first to notice us, and she hopped down from Dimitrius's lap and sprinted over to us, hugging me around my legs. The rest of the family came over to greet us.

"Seems like the odds are being stacked against you, Arthur," Loch said. "Better for me when you win."

"You're betting on the race?" I asked, half amused and half aghast.

"Hell yeah. Hey, it's not just me. Mason, too. And about half of the masters at school."

Mason smiled, sheepishly. "We all think you're going to win," he said, encouragingly.

"Be *careful*," Stella said to Arthur, brushing a bit of fluff from his shoulder. "I don't know if I'll even be able to watch."

"I'll be fine, Mom," he said.

. . .

Basch gripped his son's shoulder. "I have no doubt you'll race well, Arthur. Make the clan proud."

"I will."

Guided by the track manager, we made our way down to the garage bays at track-side. Eyes were on us from everywhere, and we received words of support from all sorts of people we passed by along the way.

"This is crazy," Arthur said.

"It feels like everyone knows about us," I agreed. "No pressure."

"Nothing has changed. Now we just have an audience. I'm still going to race the same."

We went into the garage bays, and the other riders came over from their bikes to wish us a good race. Then, as we made our way down the line towards Arthur's electric blue wolf-cycle, Gregor emerged from behind his bike. He was using his XR76 'Rip Jaw', its neon-orange body covered in sponsorship stickers. He was flirting with a young omega, and grinned when he noticed us.

. . .

"May the best wolf win," Arthur said, offering his hand. Gregor ignored it.

"I think it's obvious who that is." He spat onto the floor next to Arthur's feet. He stabbed a glare at me. "I'll see *you* very soon."

"You'll be seeing the last of me, Gregor," I said. Without another word, Arthur and I strode past him.

"He's got no chance!" Gregor yelled after us. "Don't even think for a second he's going to win. Perry! I'm talking to you!"

We made our way down the line, until we reached the end where Arthur's bike was. He laid his hand against its side and closed his eyes for a moment. "Time to do this," he said. On monitors hanging from the garage ceiling was video feed of the race currently happening on the track. Arthur changed into his racing suit and then the two of us walked around his bike to do an inspection. We both worked in silence, too nervous to talk. My heart was pounding so hard, I almost couldn't feel my legs. Everything was tingling, and I felt like I was on the verge of vomiting, even though I hadn't had the appetite to eat a bite of anything the entire day. Arthur was the same, and I was worried if he'd have trouble because of it. I knew whatever I was feeling, he had to be having it worse. But when I looked at him, his eyes were surprisingly calm. He sat on the ground next to his bike, his back against it. He stared straight ahead, his hands folded in his lap. I sat down facing him, and he smiled at me.

"Thinking about the race," I said. It wasn't really a question, but to my surprise, Arthur said, "No."

"Names," he said.

"Names?"

"What we should name our baby. If it's a boy, maybe Mars. A girl, Venus. Something from the stars, like Jupiter."

I smiled, moved that he was thinking about something like that at a time like this. But then, maybe it was the best time to think about it. Anything to focus, to keep the nerves calm.

"From the stars," I agreed.

We sat quietly together, Arthur's hands resting in my palms. His pulse was steady, and it helped to calm me. A short time later, we were approached by the track manager.

"Your race is next," he said.

. . .

We stood, our hands still clasped. I looked into Arthur's eyes, willing him as much strength as I could, but I could see he didn't need it. He was focused. He was ready. He slipped his hand around my waist and pulled me into a kiss.

"This is it," he whispered.

I kissed him again, and a part of me wondered if it might be the last time. I felt a pulling urge to grab his hand and run. I didn't want to lose him again.

"Kick his ass," I said.

His lips formed a slanted smile. Slowly, reluctantly, he let go of my hand. "Talk to you on the track," he said, and then shifted into wolf form. I hurried off towards the pit, and heard the grumbling roar of his engine behind me as he started his bike and pulled out of the garage.

ARTHUR

I pulled my bike out onto the track and to the starting line. Gregor's orange monstrosity was already there, taunting me with its sheer excess. He'd purposely chosen his competitive bike to try and intimidate me, to remind me that he was a pro and I was not. I wasn't worried. Any worry that I'd had before was gone now, thanks to Perry's news. I was fighting for one more, now: my own child.

I couldn't see Gregor through the tinted cockpit window, but I knew he was looking at me, goading me on. I remembered the practice races, and how he wielded his own overconfidence as a weapon against weaker opponents. I could use that against him, if I didn't fall to it first.

"Perry here," his voice crackled over the radio. "Here comes the rain."

. . .

Just as he said that, specks of water spotted the windshield. I hit a button, and a light flashed across the glass, adding an augmented view that electronically removed any rain from my view. I wouldn't be inhibited visually, but racing on a wet track would still be different, no matter how many assistance electronics the bikes had.

"No problem," I said. Through the controls, I felt the shudder of the engine through my paws. I revved the throttle a bit, letting myself get in tune with the bike.

"The announcer is introducing your race now," Perry said. I couldn't hear anything except him and the immediate sounds of my engine. "Hounds of Hell. You should hear the crowd right now. Alright, Arthur. Here we go. Get ready for the lights."

Gregor started to rev his bike, its engine spitting jets of flame from the twin exhaust. The bike shook with each rev, like an angry beast wanting to escape a pen. Asshole would do anything for intimidation. I ignored him, focusing on the track ahead. I took a few deep breaths and quieted my mind.

For Perry.

For Jupiter.

For our baby.

. . .

The signal lights appeared on my heads-up display.

Red.

Yellow.

GREEN!

Throttle, clutch, the explosive force of takeoff. My engine screamed as the numbers on my speedometer climbed with blistering speed, the world around me pulling to a streaked blur with Gregor to my right. No ghost, this time. The real deal. I could feel the force of the rain through my controls, and the way the tires responded to the now slickened pavement. I gritted my teeth, gravity tugging on my chops as I blasted through the first turn. Gregor was on the inside. When we emerged from the corner, he pulled up aggressively, coming within a few feet of me. A red collision warning message flashed on my display.

"Shit," I growled. I knew what he was trying to do. He wanted me to flinch, to swerve away from him. I held the course.

"Bastard," Perry said.

. . .

"Yes he is," I said.

"Upcoming turn. Reduce by thirty. Watch your three o'clock. Don't let him intimidate you."

"Copy that," I said, and followed his instructions into the turn. Gregor again edged close to me, so much so that I could actually feel the report of water jetted from his tires vibrating against the side of my bike. My heart hammered. *Hounds of Hell, he came close.* How fucking close was he willing to get to me?

Don't let him psych you out, I told myself.

"Here comes the first obstacle," Perry said, "Get ready. The dangerous part starts now."

PERRY

The skies had opened up. The sound of the rain hammering down was almost as loud as the roar of the crowd as Arthur and Gregor pulled into the first obstacle, a winding tunnel with no flat surfaces, just a pure cylinder that forced the drivers to ride up along the sides, or even on the ceiling at times. I watched as Gregor did a three hundred and sixty flip around the tunnel, arcing around the ceiling to come onto the opposite side of Arthur. It was a completely unnecessary move. The piece of shit was so arrogant, he was *toying* with Arthur. It made me furious, and I could see that it was beginning to get to Arthur.

"Ignore him, Arthur," I said. "Ignore him."

"Fuck," he said. I watched as Arthur pulled the same move, whirling around the ceiling to put Gregor back on his right side.

. . .

"Arthur, don't," I said. "Don't let him get to you."

"He's making it really difficult," he replied. "Dammit!"

Gregor had forced him slightly onto the side of the tunnel. Because the tunnel was perfectly round, when the obstacle ended both racers needed to be running along the bottom in order to safely emerge onto flat ground. That usually meant a game of chicken, with one rider edging the other out and exiting first. Arthur jerked his bike towards Gregor, trying to get him up the side of the of the tunnel, but he didn't budge. They were both in a dangerous position, the question was who would be the one to pull back? This was one of the moments that I couldn't do anything to help Arthur. He would have to decide on a strategy himself.

I chewed my lip. He was getting closer to the end of the tunnel, and was still riding side by side with Gregor. Gregor was still in the safe position, and Arthur's attempts to get him to move were not working. He attempted to pull ahead of him, but the winding curves of the tunnel were preventing him from picking up much more speed. He was stuck.

"Come on, Arthur," I whispered to myself. Through his cockpit feed I could see the intense look of concentration on his face, burning behind his wolf eyes. "Come on..."

. . .

I could see the end of the tunnel coming up fast ahead. It was obvious that Gregor had the upper position. He wasn't going to be psyched out. What was Arthur going to do?

Drop back, I thought. *Before it's too late!* But he wasn't. He continued to ride the side of the tunnel, and they were hurtling towards the exit.

Here it came!

"Arthur!" I shouted.

At the last second, he whipped his bike in a loop around the top of the tunnel, accelerating at the very last moment before he reached the end. His bike shot ahead of Gregor's *along the ceiling*, and with the momentum of the move he flew out from the exit over Gregor's bike and landed just ahead of him on the track! Smoke puffed from his tires as he landed, the back of his bike wobbling to regain traction as water exploded off the track into a fine mist. The crowd burst into a roar of applause, and I threw my arms in the air.

"Fuck yes!"

"That was close," he said into the mic.

. . .

Gregor swerved back and forth, trying to find a way to pull ahead of him, but Arthur moved with him, blocking his attempts. I could only imagine how furious he must've been right now. But it was way too early to get relaxed. They pulled into a turn and Gregor started to edge in along the left side. He was driving even more aggressively now, no longer toying around. They came out of the turn neck and neck again, hurtling towards the next obstacle.

The narrow loops of the Dog's Eye were even more treacherous in the rain, notorious for flinging overly-confident riders when they took their bikes too close to the edge. I reminded Arthur about this, giving him the track conditions that were scrolling along the bottom of my screen. They increased their speed and pulled into the first and smallest of the loops, flying around it without any issue. The second loop was larger in size, but the track also became narrower, forcing the bikes closer together. Gregor jerked his bike quickly to the right and *actually tapped the side of Arthur's.* The man was insane! He could make them both crash, doing that!

"Son of a bitch," Arthur growled. "Damn him."

The second time Gregor went in for a tap, Arthur suddenly decreased his speed, dropping back behind Gregor's bike. Gregor didn't expect it, and his bike shot dangerously close to the edge of the track. They entered the loop and flew around it, and when they exited, Arthur used the slingshot momentum to drive him back forward and even the position with Gregor once again.

. . .

"Maybe he'll stop fucking around with me, now," Arthur grumbled.

"Don't count on it," I said.

They entered a series of zig-zagging curves, and their bikes smashed through the film of rainwater sitting on the surface of the tarmac and made it jet up hundreds of feet in the air. Arthur cursed and fell behind Gregor as he pumped on his brakes.

"Damn controls feel like they're shaking apart under my paws. The water on the track..."

"You're fine," I reassured him. "Keep your speed up."

He accelerated, coming up on Gregor's side again. Their bikes swerved through the turns in unison, like fighters exchanging blows. Just ahead was the next obstacle, The Walls, but both of our minds were on the final obstacle, The Forest. With these conditions, we both knew just how much more treacherous it would be.

ARTHUR

I was still holding my own against Gregor, and I don't think he expected that. The balance of power had shifted. He now knew that those little tricks he tried playing on me at the start of the race weren't going to work, and was now racing seriously against me. I could feel the fury in his driving. It was aggressive, but precise. He would push it to the edge, and in order to beat him, I would have to also. I couldn't afford to make a single mistake.

"You're fine," Perry said. "Keep your speed up."

Hearing his words encouraged me. I knew I could rely on him. It was one less thing to have to think about. I increased speed, ignoring the reflex of fear as the controls vibrated from the water on the track.

. . .

I needed as much speed as possible for The Walls, in order to maintain grip in a vertical position. I could see the obstacle just ahead, coming up fast. Then, Gregor accelerated and pulled ahead of me. I did the same. He tried to block me from gaining more speed, but I wasn't going to have it. Instead of slowing to avoid hitting his rear tire, I accelerated and bumped into it. Our bikes wiggled violently, and I managed to correct it. Gregor did too, and quickly pulled away from me, taking the left path. I took the right, and we both curved up onto the parallel walls, riding completely vertically.

I could feel the rain water gushing down the sides of walls. My pulse raced. Did I have enough speed to maintain this? Had I just fucked myself over? I glanced up and saw Gregor on the opposite wall. His bike was slowly drifting down. We were both having trouble maintaining traction.

"Tilt down," Perry said calmly. "Use gravity."

I realized he was right. I made a quick calculation in my head and then let the bike drift down the wall as I kept on the accelerator. My downward trajectory gave me enough speed to maintain traction and keep me up on the wall. I saw that Gregor had gotten the same idea, too. Right before my bike was about to drop off the wall, we hit the end of the obstacle, and the track curved back horizontally and put me back upright. The tracks re-combined, and Gregor appeared back on my left side.

"Thanks," I said to Perry.

. . .

"This is it. Final stretch. Increase by ten. Full speed into The Forest."

I was surprised. He'd always been conservative about The Forest, advising me to enter cautiously. "Full speed," I repeated.

"You can do it."

I grinned and hit the accelerator. Gregor had the same thought, and matched my speed. It seemed like the race was going to come down a matter of milliseconds. Neither of us had budged at all.

I'm going to win this. Perry and I will be together. We're going to have our baby together.

I entered the last straightaway, and the world streaked past my windshield, a brilliant blur. As my speedometer climbed to its max, I felt that amazing sensation of excited calm that I could only get when at such speeds. It was a high, the flirtation of being on the verge of losing control. This used to be the ultimate sensation, one of the reasons why I raced. Now I realized that I didn't need it anymore. I had something so much better. Every moment I spent with Perry was more thrilling than this.

. . .

Ahead, I saw the towering concrete pylons of The Forest. This was it.

I entered. Perry had gone silent to let me concentrate. I edged as close as possible to the pylons to avoid having to make costly, speed-sacrificing corrections with my trajectory.

My screen flashed red with a sudden collision warning, and I turned to see Gregor hurtling towards me from the side.

"What the fuck!"

I jerked the controls and dropped my speed just enough for him to fly past me. He curved around the oncoming pylons and came back at me on the other side, again aiming to hit me.

"Arthur!" Perry shouted. "That bastard is trying to knock you out!"

I swerved around a pylon, using it as a shield and forcing Gregor to split away from his attack. He came again, and I just barely dodged him and came within spitting distance of a pylon.

"Shit," I said. "He's insane."

. . .

Red filled my screen, and Gregor seemed to emerge from nowhere, flying towards me as the pylons whizzed by. I tried to avoid him, but his front tire impacted my rear tire, sending me into a spin.

Perry shouted, "No!"

The world blurred around me. I knew I had seconds to react. I pushed the brake and jammed down on the controls, switching to reverse. I engaged the throttle, and my bike emerged from its spin—backwards. I was driving backwards through the course.

"Shit, shit, shit," I muttered, swerving around the oncoming pylons. Gregor was just up ahead. I accelerated, and came up on his side, still riding backwards. I could only imagine the shock and fury he must've had seeing me come up on him riding in reverse. He brought his bike at me again, but this time I was ready. I hit the brake and swung my bike. My tires screeched as I spun back around, and his wheel narrowly missed hitting mine. I was facing straight again and I narrowly avoided a blur of oncoming pylons, moving my bike around them with the slightest turns. I gritted my teeth as one grazed me.

Gregor had not been so lucky. When I'd dodged his attack, he'd flung by me and just barely clipped the side of a pylon. He was fighting to get control over his wobbling bike now.

. . .

"Eject," I whispered. "You maniac, you're going to crash."

In my side monitor I could see him barely missing the pylons. He'd been thrown off his rhythm. There was no recovering.

Then he hit one! His bike spun along the track. Somehow, he managed to regain control and right himself, but he was heading straight for a pylon. I turned my eyes away and gunned my engine. The edge of The Forest was just ahead.

I could feel the force of the explosion behind me, and warning alarms chimed as debris hurtled across the track. I avoided the last pylon but a hunk of debris skipped across the tarmac ahead of me. I jerked the steering, but another piece struck my side. I lost control. My bike slammed on its side and started to spin across the ground. I saw Gregor's crash behind me in strobing flashes as my bike spun. The curl of black smoke, the fire, the mangled bike.

"Arthur!" Perry shouted. "Arthur! Deploy your chute!"

I activated my emergency stop parachute and my bike jerked violently. I could see sparks flying up around me and a trail of thick, grey smoke. With the aid of the chute, my bike slid to a stop. Red warning lights flashed and the alarm continued to sound. The engine had died in the crash, so I cut the electronics and hit the door release. Nothing happened. The cockpit began to fill with acrid smoke. I released my paws from the control modules and hammered the door with my leg. *Shit!* It was jammed! I shifted back to human form and scrambled to look for the manual release lever. The smoke was so thick! I couldn't breathe!

Suddenly, there was a hiss, and the door flew open. Rain cut through the smoke, spattering my face with cold relief. Hands grabbed me and yanked me out, and I stumbled onto the wet pavement, my eyes burning and watering from the smoke. I looked back and could just barely make out the smoking heap that was my bike. Orange flames emerged from the side, and it was soon engulfed in fire. I turned back, the rescue crew helping me off the track. Sirens wailed in the distance. I saw a blurry figure running towards me. I wiped my eyes, and somehow the mixture of tears and rain water cleared my vision. It was Perry.

He threw his arms around me, hugging me so tight I could barely breathe. It was a good feeling. I was alive.

"I crashed," I said, weakly.

"You *won*," he said. A firetruck pulled up and started to douse my bike with water, and it was at that moment that I saw what had happened. A blackened trail across the asphalt traced the path my bike had skidded after I'd crashed—across the finish line. I'd slid across the finish line.

. . .

I did it. I won.

The rain continued to pour down, soaking us. As my senses slowly returned, and I realized that the crowd was on their feet, cheering, Perry took my face into his hands and kissed me. The cheers turned into a roar. It felt like I was still traveling at top speed, like everything was a blur around me. I kissed Perry. I felt his body against mine, his hands on my cheeks, the taste of his lips. He was free.

"We gotta get you off the track!" a rescue crewman said, running up to us and ushering us off the tarmac, where my bike was smoldering.

"Right," I said, still in a stunned haze.

"Houndfang is fine," he said. "Thought you might want to know. He's being transported to a healing clinic now."

I may have hated his guts, but I was glad he'd survived that horrific crash. In the end, he'd caused his own defeat by trying to sabotage me. He must've come to the same conclusion that I had: the winner was going to be decided by a matter of milliseconds. That possibility of defeat must've been too much for him to handle.

We made it under the cover of the garage pits. Someone wrapped towels around us. Hands slapped my back in congratulations. All I wanted to do was get out of there, to just be with my mate.

"Arthur! Perry!"

Our family was running towards us. Jupiter hopped down from Dimitrius's arms and reached us first. We scooped her up into our arms, and she hugged me around my neck.

"You won, Papa?" she asked.

"I won, Jupiter," I said. "I won."

PERRY

We didn't wait long to make our union official. Two days after the race, Arthur and I were wed in a small ceremony held in the apple orchard behind the Luna estate, with only our immediate family in attendance. After the ceremony, I announced that Arthur and I were going to be having a baby.

That night, we snuck away from the house while all the rest of the family was partying. After everything that'd we'd gone through, we just needed some time alone together to let it all sink in. So we headed to the old race track. It just seemed to be the obvious place to go.

We were surprised to find the track was being used by a group of young, wannabe racers, so we quietly made our way up to the announcer's box to watch them. They zipped around the track, their bikes like flitting fireflies in the darkness. Arthur put his arm around me and hugged me close, our legs dangling off the roof of the building. I rested my hands in his, and he gently touched the wedding band that was around my finger. A stillness came over me then, like the moment of peace before drifting off to sleep. Today was the first day of our lives together. It was still hard for me to imagine. It didn't feel quite real, but we were together. Married and mated. Alpha and omega.

"I'm quitting wolf-cycle racing," Arthur announced, suddenly. "That was my last race."

"But you love to race."

"I'll always love the sport. But I don't need to race anymore. Whatever happiness racing gave me is nothing compared to the happiness I feel when I'm with you. It's served its purpose. I'm done with it. And especially with our baby coming." He smiled. "I'm ready to move on."

"We made a hell of a team," I said.

He kissed me. "We still do."

The sound of the bikes on the track drifted up to us like calls from the past, one that had already begun to slip away. All the pain and the wounds of our time apart would heal now, and we would create new memories together as mates and as family.

"Perry Luna," Arthur whispered to me. "I'll love you forever."

EPILOGUE - PERRY

Mars was born only two months after his cousin Malcolm, so Arthur and I would take turns switching off with Tresten and Loch on babysitting duty. Stella and Basch helped out a lot, too. Arthur and I had decided not to leave the Luna estate like his siblings, and our family lived with his parents. They were thankful to have the company, and it was nice to have their assistance.

Jupiter especially loved the house. She could spend hours on her own, exploring the different wings, having all sorts of little adventures. And of course, her cousins came to visit often. She and Alexis were so close, they were practically sisters.

In the year since the race, Gregor had only attempted to reach out to me once, via phone. The call reached the Luna house, but I refused to take it. I found out later that the publicity generated by the challenge had put him and his clan in a negative light as people found out about the reason for the challenge. Then, it was outed that he'd had children with at least four others besides me, both women and omegas, while we were married. Apparently it became a scandal in Elclaw, and his clan had voted to remove him from their ranks. He'd also badly injured his leg in the crash, and couldn't operate a wolf-cycle anymore.

Life moved on. Unable to entirely quit the racing life, Arthur decided to open up a training school for hopeful racers, where we both became instructors. Many of the students who came to the school were familiar with who we were, and they wanted to hear about the challenge for love first hand. We were always happy to retell the story.

Love had guided us. It had brought Arthur victory. Love was the power that could move mountains and save souls. It was the most powerful force in the universe. In the thirteen years apart, our love had never died. We knew that even if all the time in the world had passed, it still would've remained as an ember deep in our hearts, just waiting to be lit again.

Want more of Arthur and Perry?
Download a special FREE bonus chapter, "*First Meeting*"!
Keep turning till the very end of the book for the download link.

And if you enjoyed *Bound to the Omega*, please consider leaving a rating or review. All positive encouragement is a great help to authors! You can easily access the product page by scanning the QR code with your phone.

Loch's Story - Wed to the Omega
Vander's Story - Doctor to the Omega
Christophe's Story - Marked to the Omega

Looking for something similar to the Luna Brothers? Check out The Dragon Firefighters series!

*"A surprising adventure and decisions affect more than one life and the town. Great story. **Absolutely wonderful characters.**"*

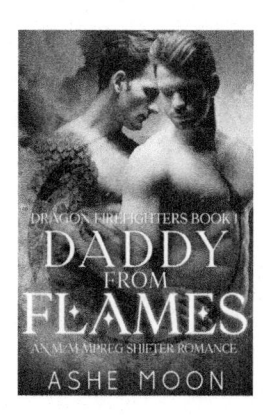

Pregnant and without an alpha, human omega Grayson must rely on his tenacity to provide for his unborn daughter. But when a fire claims his home and everything he's struggled to work for, rescue comes in an unexpected form: the alpha dragon Altair and his flight of firefighters who reluctantly take Grayson into their custody.

Altair's resentment of humanity is matched by a conflicting sense of duty to protect the town they share and all who call it home, human or dragon. He and his flight brothers have never had to deal with an omega before—let alone a human—and now they have one living under their roof! Everything Altair thought he knew about humans, omegas, and mates is called into question—and with Grayson's baby on the way, he's about to find out what it's like to be a daddy.

Daddy From Flames is the first book in the Dragon Firefighters mpreg series. This book features dragon shifters, a human omega, firefighters, an industrial fantasy setting, pregnancy/birth, new dads, a cat, love healing wounds, action, fun, light drama, and, as always, a happily ever after.

Scan the QR code with your phone camera to see the entire series!

FREE BONUS CHAPTER

Scan the QR code to sign up for my mailing list and receive *"First Meeting"*, the **FREE bonus chapter** to *Bound to the Omega*!

FREE BONUS CHAPTER

First Edition Cover

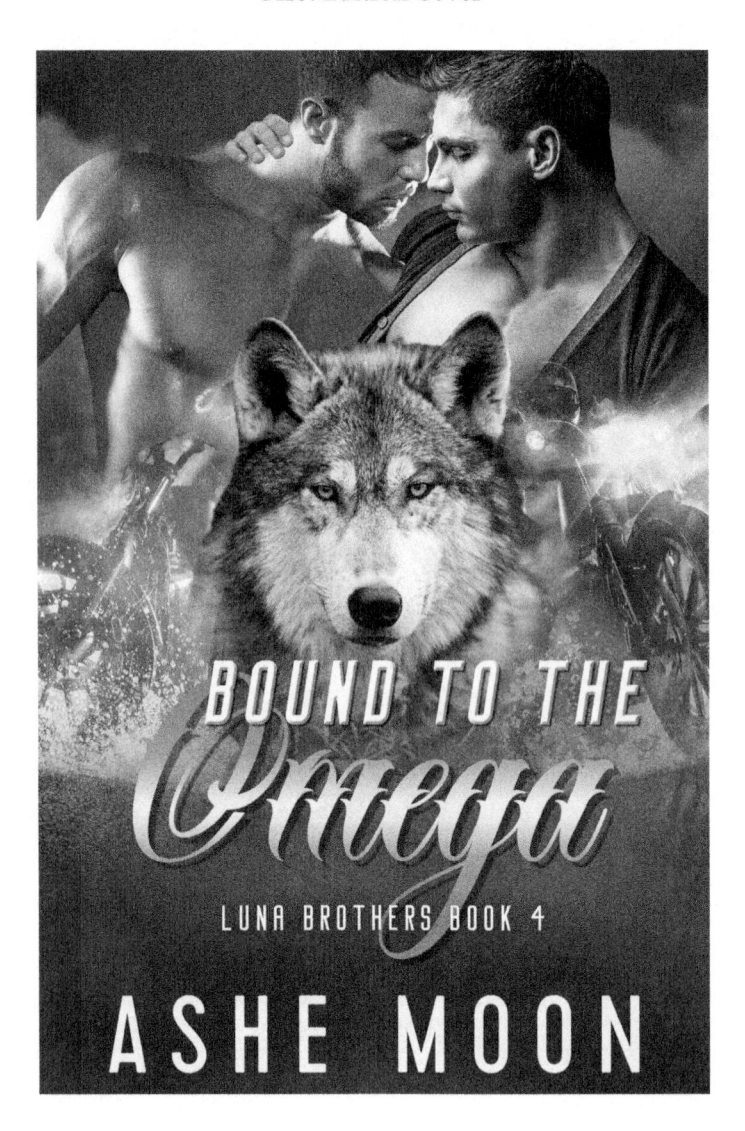

Printed in Great Britain
by Amazon